FINDING PONY

Horizon Bound Books, an imprint of HBE Publishing, is proud to issue this edition of Finding Pony as our inaugural publication. It is limited to 110 hardbound copies. Ten copies are identified as Publisher Presentation and lettered A-J and signed by the author and publisher. The remaining 100 are numbered and signed by the author.

This is copy: _I_

FINDING PONY

FINDING PONY

KARA LUCAS

HORIZON BOUND BOOKS

CLOVIS, CALIFORNIA

FINDING PONY. Copyright © 2015 Kara Lucas

Horizon Bound Books
An Imprint of HBE Publishing

All inquiries should be addressed to:
HBE Publishing
640 Clovis Ave
Clovis, CA, 93612
http://www.hbepublishing.com

Library of Congress Control Number: 2015940643

ISBN 978-1-943050-02-4 HARDBACK, LIMITED EDITION
ISBN 978-1-943050-03-1 TRADE PAPERBACK
ISBN 978-1-943050-04-8 EBOOK

Printed in the United States of America
September 2015

HBE PUBLISHING

For Z,C,K,C,L and M.
Always.

One

tweaker pad (n): a place, usually a home or apartment, inhabited by methamphetamine users.

The TV glowed blue in the darkness. Our trailer was quiet except for the tinny echo of David Hasselhoff's voice and Pony as she slurped her grape soda through a straw.

"Pone, can't you be quieter?" I nudged her. "I'm trying to listen."

"Sorry." She scraped the last bit of ramen noodles from the Styrofoam cup. "Can I have more?"

"Nope. That's it."

"Oh. That's okay." She grabbed her pink stuffed horse and clutched it to her chest, rubbing the frayed ear with her cheek. "I thought Mom said we had no food."

"Mom doesn't know everything." I forced a smile. Darryl would kill me if he found out I lifted from him—even if it was only a couple of bucks.

She leaned her head on my shoulder. "You're the best big

brother ever."

"I'm your only brother, brat. Now quit talking. Let's watch the show." I focused on the screen, the scene a perfect beach with the hottest girls I'd ever seen wearing red bathing suits that were tight in all the right places. I'd never seen the ocean, but I was sure it was just like the show. Blue and enormous. Peaceful. I closed my eyes and imagined the way the waves would sound crashing around me.

"Do you think Mom'll come home tonight?"

"No."

She'd been gone for about three days. I had to miss school so someone would be home with Pony. But like all the other times, I knew that eventually Mom and Darryl would come home when the meth ran out, and then they'd crash for days.

"Jesse?"

I sighed. "What?"

"Is it real? Do people really live like that? On the beach, wearing bathing suits all the time?"

"Yeah. Sure."

Her face scrunched up. "I don't believe you."

"You calling your brother a liar? It's all true." I watched her eyelids grow heavy. "That's Malibu. Everyone lives on the beach, even the little kids. They sell ice cream on the sand, and there's a Ferris wheel and merry-go-round, right on the beach."

"Right on the beach? Can we go?"

"Not now. Someday, like when you turn five. Maybe, when I'm a famous artist, we'll even live there."

"...In bathing suits?" She yawned and closed her eyes.

"Sure. In bathing suits."

She snuggled against me, and I could feel the bony point of

her elbow dig into my side. Within a minute she was asleep, her chest rising and falling in shallow, rhythmic breaths.

I stared back at the flickering screen. *Just another exciting Friday night for Jesse Sampson.*

*   *   *

I must have fallen asleep sometime during the second Baywatch. All I know is I was having the best dream in my whole life. I was surfing in Malibu, like I'd been surfing for years. My board was shredding down this huge half-pipe when it crashed. The salty waves were all around me; I couldn't breathe and struggled to swim toward the light. Out of nowhere one of the girls—the hottest blond one—-rescued me, and said that she had to perform mouth-to-mouth resuscitation. I said okay (not saying no), but I was breathing fine, and she said, just shut up Jesse, and then we started kissing like crazy, and I was so into it, and then—

Knock knock knock.

My eyes flew open.

When your stepdad's a drug dealer, there are only two reasons that someone would knock on your piece of crap trailer in the middle of the night: drugs or cops.

Knock knock knock.

Junkies aren't usually so demanding. They rap very quietly, and creep through the back door by the kitchen, so I'm thinking that this must be cops.

Holy shit. The cops.

I rolled off my mattress, and fumbled for Pony's bed in the

darkness.

"Jesse?" She yawned and rubbed her eyes with a fist.

"Shhh. Someone's here. Cops."

My heart thumped in my chest as I heard the knock again, louder this time. I reached under her bed, yanking out dirty clothes and trash. Trying to make room. Through the thin paneled walls I could hear the front door opening and Mom's voice.

"Jesse, I think I hear Mom——"

"Shhh!" I picked her up, it was like lifting a feather, and stuffed her under the bed, piling the clothes on top.

"What are you doing?"

"Hiding you. Look—stay put, you hear? Whatever you do, don't move."

"Aren't you hiding, too?" Her voice was a whimper.

I was panting, terror snaking through my gut. There wasn't enough room. I'd be caught. We both would be.

The conversation was muffled through the closed door and I could hear the police officer's heavy boots shift in the living room. Mom sobbing. Metal handcuffs, clinking against each other. A softer, female voice—probably the social worker, was calm, soothing.

"Any minors in the house, ma'am?"

It was almost too late. Frantically, I shoved a final filthy blanket around her. "Remember what I said," I whispered.

"Jesse, don't leave me," she begged.

"I have to." I spoke to the pile of clothing and stuck a hand underneath, giving her arm a quick final squeeze. "I'll come back for you."

I raced to the window; it squeaked and shuddered as I pushed it open. The bedroom vibrated with three strong knocks. "Police. Unlock the door."

My knees banged as I hoisted myself up and crouched on the windowsill. The aluminum cut into my bare feet. I jumped onto the hard dirt and took off toward the river. Tumbleweeds scratched my legs, and with every gulp of air my mind registered only one thing: Pony.

I thought of her hiding there in the dirty laundry, scared and alone. I just left her to fend for herself. In her four years, she had never been taken away, never been in foster care. Not like me.

I could puke with the guilt, but my legs kept moving. Either instinct or fear—it didn't matter. I just couldn't do it.

I couldn't get taken again.

TWO

up shit creek (phr): to be in deep trouble with
no solution.

A beam of hot June sunlight filtered through a sycamore branch and scorched my eyelids. Hidden in a pile of leaves and sagebrush next to the riverbank, I hadn't slept more than a couple hours all night. My eyes were bleary and tight and my tongue screamed with thirst. Now I knew how tweakers felt.

I drank some water from the river and spotted our trailer. It perched on the edge of the river like an empty shoebox.

Please. Please be there.

The trailer park was quiet with sleep. I slunk around toward the front and my stomach dropped. Yellow crime-scene tape crisscrossed the front door. The landlord had tacked a homemade note on the grimy window: *Keep Out.*

I jiggled the knob. The door creaked open.

Our living room smelled of body odor and rotting food. My

footsteps echoed on the cracked linoleum.

"Pony?"

The door to our room was flung wide. The blanket Pony had been wrapped in was still underneath the bed. I allowed myself the tiniest sliver of hope.

"Pony!" I shot over and with both arms squeezed the blanket to my body.

There was nothing but air.

Like a baby, I sobbed in my trashed, empty room for what seemed like forever. And then I was pissed at myself for crying, because I was the one who did it to her. I was the one who left the helpless kid all by herself. I could guess what happened to Mom and Darryl, but Pony—I couldn't even think about it.

Her stuffed horse lay on the ground. How was she going to go to bed without it? She slept with that thing every single night. I clutched it to me and lay on my side, curling up into a ball. Not even the sound of the river, the only nice thing about living in Bravo Hills Trailer Park, could comfort me. I knew I was a piece of shit.

*   *   *

Sometime later, a scraping, shuffling sound in the living room made me prick my ears. Someone was inside the trailer. Crazy thoughts gripped me. Maybe it was the police come back to get me. Or Mom. Maybe it was Pony, hiding in a different part of the trailer.

I raced into the living room.

Merlin, our next-door neighbor, was dragging our TV towards the front door. His long greasy hair hung into his face, and his shirt lifted in the back, exposing pale, pasty skin.

Red rage boiled inside me. *The fricking nerve.* Without thinking, I lunged for him. The TV skidded across the room. I pinned him to the floor.

"Dude!" He gasped and clutched at his throat.

"What did you do with her? Where is she?" My hands were around his neck, but I was removed from it all, as if I were watching myself in a movie. His eyes bugged out and my adrenaline surged. I smelled his stinking, pot breath as I squeezed harder, and harder.

"Jesse," he croaked, his face now purple. "What's wrong with you? You tweaking or what?"

His words snapped me back into reality. Horrified, I loosened my grip on his neck and rolled off of him, cradling my head in my hands. I felt sick. Maybe I was a piece of shit, but I wasn't a murderer.

"Sorry. God. I'm sorry."

He coughed and rubbed his throat. "You could have killed me, man." His pale eyes were wide and accusing. "It's like you're on 'roids. Are you on 'roids? Aren't you only like twelve or something?" His fingers were thin, with long, jagged nails.

"Fifteen. And I couldn't have killed you."

"We've been friends since we were little, and then you go and attack me."

"Friends" was a loose term, to say the least. Merlin was three years older than me and lived with his dad, a vet with one leg. His parents were way into witchcraft, but ever since his mom split, he and his dad just played video games all day, and only left their trailer to hit the WinCo for food.

His voice gave me a headache. "Friends don't creep in their friends' houses and steal their TVs, okay?" I said, glaring over. The black box rested on its side against the wall.

He sniffed. "It's not your TV any more, bro. Lenny said you guys were three months behind on rent. He's gonna sell all your crap anyway."

I wiped my face with my hands. Darryl wasn't the most successful drug dealer. You usually aren't when you use most of your product. Through the open door, I saw the yellow tape flutter in the breeze and struggled to fill in the blanks.

"What happened?" I asked finally.

"Your mom? She's toast, man. Busted, big time." He let out a high-pitched cackle. "You know what went down? She and Darryl. They held up the minimart on Fifth. Armed freakin' robbery." He practically savored each word. "Lenny says they're in County right now, but they'll do hard time for this one."

My fingers went numb. Mom had never tried to hurt anyone before. She couldn't. Sure, she had been arrested a few times for possession, like the year I spent in foster care, but she always managed to stay out of serious trouble.

"They don't even have a gun," I whispered.

He smiled and bared his yellow teeth. "No. A knife. From some other tweaker's kitchen." He shook his head. "Dude. Big time."

"What happened to Pony?" My throat caught when I said her name.

"You know the drill. CPS took her."

Child Protective Services. I already knew, but I needed him to say it. "You saw?"

"Uh-huh. But it was the nice one, the redhead. Wilma, I think. She was hugging her and stuff."

At least I could be grateful for that. I was eight the night CPS took me away. My social worker was young and pretty, and bought me a Happy Meal. Her name was Mandy, she had just gotten married and she smelled like marshmallows. I hadn't showed up for school in a week—Mom was on a bender, and my teacher called CPS. Mandy came and took me, promising that I would come back if she got clean and learned how to be a good mommy. I remembered sitting on Mandy's lap, resting my head against her soft chest while I ate my fries.

"I have a little boy your age," she whispered into my hair. "He likes to play baseball."

I cried because I was scared, but when I smelled her marshmallow smell and saw how pretty her nails looked—pink and shiny, like a seashell—I felt a longing I never knew existed. I thought, *I could be your little boy, maybe. Take me away, and I could be your boy.*

Merlin craned his head to look outside. "They'll be looking for you, too, you know."

The social workers. I guess I was a dependent of the county, now. A runaway dependent at that. All I wanted to do was curl up on my mattress and sleep. And forget. I ran my fingers through my hair.

"What are you going to do?" Merlin flicked his eyes over at me and shrugged. "I guess—I guess you could crash with us for a while."

"No thanks." I glanced at his shorts. Wait. It was a long shot, but I could at least try. "Let me see your phone."

"Aw, no Jess, I've only got like five minutes left on it. Go up to Fifth and use the pay phone."

I gritted my teeth. "You were about to take my TV, you stoner. The least you can do is let me use your phone."

He gave an exaggerated sigh. "Fine." He reached inside his pocket and tossed it.

I punched in the numbers, praying my memory was right.

On the third ring, a familiar female voice picked up. "Hello?"

"Aunt Darla?"

"Jesse? Is that you? Are you okay? I heard Annette was in County."

"So you know."

"Yeah, I got a call about 3:00 in the morning from a social worker, wanting to know if I'd take you guys in."

My heart beat faster. "You have Pony? Is she okay? I want to talk to her."

"No, I don't have her yet. She's in whatchamacallit, emergency foster care. They have to investigate me or something. But I told them I would."

"Really?" I held my breath. "Me too?"

"Yeah, well, we're family. I told them I'd take the both of you. As long as you stay out of my hair."

My breath came in quick, fast puffs. "Listen, Aunt Darla, you don't have to worry about a thing. I don't party and I get good grades. Well, kind of. Pony's real good too and I mostly take care of her. It'll be great, you'll see. I can help you with the chores and maybe even get a part-time job."

"Cool," she interrupted. "Look, I gotta go to work. But you'll have to get here yourself. Can you find a ride?"

Darla went to community college in Long Beach. I had no idea where that was. Somewhere by Los Angeles. But hell yes, I could find a way to Long Beach. I exhaled in relief. Pony was probably on her way there right now. Maybe the social worker bought her a Happy Meal and let her sit on her lap. Maybe she read her a story and smoothed her hair and Pony wasn't too worried that I was gone.

Maybe everything really was going to be okay.

Three

```
homeless (adj): having no home or permanent
                        residence.
```

I tossed the phone back to Merlin, who caressed it with his thumb before he put it away. "What did she say?"

I grinned. "It's cool. My aunt's going to take me. Pony's already on her way." I was sure of it.

"Where?"

"Long Beach, on the ocean. I bet you can see the water right from her house."

"Dude. You're lucky. Is she hot?"

"She's my aunt, you moron." I felt so much better that his stupid comments didn't really bother me. But I punched him in the arm anyway. "You're sick."

"No, no, I mean like if I visited you or something," he said excitedly as he followed me into the bedroom. I found my school backpack and started picking through the clothes, throwing in the least offensively dirty ones with a toothbrush and Pony's stuffed horse.

"She's like twenty-one. In college. And she's pretty, way out of your league." I added my most prized possessions: charcoal pencils and sketch pad.

When I was ready I turned to Merlin. "You have to take me there."

He staggered back. "What? No way. My dad would kill me. I don't think the car would even make it over the Grapevine."

Nothing was going to move me off course. I was going to Long Beach. *Today.* "You have to, Merle. Look, I'll pay you," I said patiently. "You can take the TV and anything else you can find before Lenny sells it all."

He scanned the room. "There's nothing here! It's all shit, Jess. Why don't you just call CPS and turn yourself in? Then they could just take you there themselves."

"I can't trust them. Come on, for all I know, they could drive me in the other direction and throw me into a group home. It's safer to just show up there myself."

He scratched his oily scalp. "Hold on, I might have an idea. I'll be right back."

"Bring me some food," I called. I was starving. The noodles were all I ate yesterday, those and a handful of saltine crackers. I pressed my fist against my stomach and hitched up my jeans.

Would I even miss this place? I'd miss the river, and watching the herons that nested in the great oaks on the other side of its banks. I'd miss the sunsets. I'd miss school, especially my art teacher Mrs. Hamel. She'd wonder why I didn't show up on the last day. I thought of Mom and wondered if she was okay. It's always tough coming clean in jail—they don't do much for you when you're coming down. I winced. Mom. Yeah, I'd miss her too.

Merlin came loping back with a box of Froot Loops and a sloppy grin on his face. "Dude, you're set. Let's go."

We headed to his dad's orange El Camino and I grabbed the box, cramming the rainbow-colored cereal into my mouth. "You're taking me to Long Beach?"

He smiled with a strange expression on his face. "I'm getting you there."

*   *   *

Merlin pulled up alongside a park and got out of the car. "Stay here," he ordered as he headed to a cluster of whitewashed apartments. It was an older area with some rundown houses and stray dogs, but it was nowhere near as bad as my neighborhood. "I'll be back in a bit."

It was already too hot and the car reeked of marijuana, so after ten minutes I got out. I pulled my sketchbook and pencils from my bag and found a park bench. The stale cereal fossilized in my stomach. I tried not to think about food.

There were no buildings cool enough to sketch, so I started on a couple of trees. I loved the way they looked, greening up the dirty blue sky. Nothing was better than the sound of the wind moving through their leaves.

I was almost done with the large cottonwood in the distance, when I spotted a girl at the edge of the park. She was with a group of people, all carrying boxes out of a white van. She was laughing and her hair was long, brown and shiny, like a Hershey's bar that had been left in the sun. Warm and soft and sweet. *What would it be like,* I wondered, *to thread my fingers through that hair*? I bet it even smelled like chocolate.

As if on cue, she looked up and saw me staring, right at her. She smiled at me, a smile as warm and good as her hair. I ducked my head and pressed my fingernails deep into my palms, not sure if I was hungry for food or her. My eyes smarted. I wanted home, only it didn't exist anymore.

I started on another drawing, a castle. Pony used to always beg me to draw her castles and princesses and ponies. I drew the princess with long, chocolate brown hair, standing on top of a turret.

"Wow. You're very talented."

I jumped. The girl stood right behind me. "Thanks." I quickly hid the paper, embarrassed that she saw me drawing her, and flashed my best smile. I usually did okay with the ladies.

"Would you like a sandwich?" She held out a cellophane wrapped sub. It looked too good to be true. The mayo and cheese were melting against the plastic. Saliva pooled in my mouth.

"Uh, sure." I was proud of the nonchalance in my voice. Maybe she was having a picnic with her family, and noticed me. I took the sandwich and smiled again. "You come here a lot?"

"Every weekend."

"Oh. I, uh—I've never been to this park before. It's nice." *What are you doing, Jesse, trying to pick up some girl*? I heard my mind scream.

"Yeah, it is. Hope you enjoy that sandwich." Her dimples creased. "I better go." She walked like a dancer and wore a white shirt and dark jeans and had that pure, clean look, like she just stepped out of the shower. Even her light-brown skin glowed. She was perfect.

"Hey," I said as she walked away. "Come back when you're done. Talk to me."

She ducked her head. "I'll try," she said. "Bye." She threw me a soft wave.

Girls. They were so strange sometimes. Some were all over you, with that hunger in their eyes, and some felt they had to play it cool. Make you work for it. But this girl, this was the type of girl I'd work for.

I sighed and ripped the wrapping off of the sandwich. Maybe she'd come back. At least I'd get to eat.

People from the far areas of the park began coming forward, lining up behind the picnic table where all the boxes were placed. I saw the girl and a couple others reach inside and hand sandwiches to the line, one by one. I froze. The people were homeless, I realized. They had tattered clothing on, and some pushed shopping carts. All of them accepted the sandwiches with a quiet nod and thank you.

I looked down at myself. I was a mess. I was so bent on leaving that I never changed my T-shirt, which was stained with the dirt from hiding and thrashing Merlin. I wiped my face. I could feel its filth and grime.

The girl thought I was homeless.

If it wasn't so pathetic I'd laugh. Because actually, that was what I was. *Homeless.* Without a home, mother, sister, or even a piece of crap stepdad.

But not for long, I reminded myself. Probably, if not most definitely, my life would be better with Aunt Darla than it ever was here.

I stood up, grabbed my sketch pad and sandwich and walked

over to the crowd of people. There stood the girl, handing out sand-wiches with that smile on her face, dimples creasing her cheeks.

"Hey," I said, and she raised her head. "I, uh, I don't need this." I handed her back the sandwich. She looked at me with a quizzical expression. "Give it to someone who does." I walked away from her with my stomach growling. I didn't look back but knew she was watching me.

Pride could be a bitch sometimes.

"Jesse!" Finally Merlin came out of the apartment and motioned me over. "He's ready for you. Let's go."

Four

pusher (n): 1. a person or thing that pushes;
2. slang, a peddler of illegal drugs.

What do you mean, 'He's ready for me'?" I asked as we walked up the crumbling steps.

"Just trust me, man." Merlin knocked on the apartment door numbered 6. "Be cool."

All of a sudden Merlin thought he was the epitome of cool. I rolled my eyes.

A sturdy Hispanic lady wearing an apron opened the door and beckoned us in. "*Bienvenido*," she said, as if we were checking in to a hotel. "He is waiting for you."

We walked inside the tidy apartment. The woman went back to making her flour tortillas in the kitchen. There, at a long Formica table sat the one person in my life who truly scared me.

"Jesse, my man." He smiled wide but his dark eyes were cold. I got the shivers. It was Beto, the one who sold Darryl his drugs.

Beto was a real drug dealer, the kind with major connections in Los Angeles. Mexico, even. Or so I heard. "Look at you, all grown up. You're the spitting image of Annette with those pretty blue eyes. I bet the *chicas* love you."

I just stared at him. My tongue felt thick and unmoving.

He peered at me. "Something wrong with you?" Beto turned to Merlin. "He stupid? Can't he speak?"

"I can speak." I forced myself to meet his gaze.

"You ready to follow in your old man's footsteps and join the family business?" He laughed and leaned back in his chair.

"He's not my dad," I mumbled. "And, no. I'm moving in with my aunt."

"She lives in Long Beach." Merlin rubbed his palms on his jeans.

"So is he good for it?" Beto looked at Merlin.

"Good for what?" I asked.

Merlin glanced at me and wet his lips. "Sure, yeah. Aren't you, Jesse? He's good for it. We've known each other since we were kids."

"You better be." He threw a rectangular package across the table covered in brown, oil-stained paper. It was wrapped tightly in duct tape. "Or I'll come for you, puto." He flashed me a steely grin.

I yanked on Merlin's T-shirt sleeve. "I thought you were taking me to L.A."

"Me? Nah. I told you I couldn't. But I can get you there, at least Beto can." He hesitated. "Tell him."

"A simple transaction. You will take the 7:15 bus departing from Truckston to Los Angeles. I will give you money for the ticket." Beto bowed his head. "Look innocent, stay clean, and when you get there, a guy named Gonzalo will take the package out of your hands." He cracked his knuckles and folded them on the table. "He'll give you forty dollars for your trouble."

Forty whole dollars. Enough to get me to Long Beach. Enough for food and phone calls, maybe even enough to buy Pony a little present when I saw her.

"Pretty sweet deal, right Jesse? *Cour-eee-orrr service,*" Merlin sing-songed.

Courier service. For a drug dealer. The drug dealer who, in fact, gave my mom her first hit of meth. I was just a kid, but I remembered. Back then, she still had all of her teeth, her hair still glossy with youth. She was beautiful, my mom was.

"Jesse?" Merlin looked nervous, as if he might crawl out of his skin. "So whaddya say?"

How could I get to Long Beach on my own? This was Merlin's pathetic idea of helping me. And yet, it was so simple. I just had to stuff it in my backpack, sit on the bus, and give it to some guy who was going to get it anyway.

"I'll do it." I stuffed my hands in my pockets. "But I want some money up front." I was shocked by my own boldness, but I was starving. My head felt light with hunger.

Beto laughed again, exposing white teeth. "You have some balls. I like it." He raised his eyebrows. "You sure you don't want to just come back and work for me? There's a job opening now, you know." He chuckled at his own joke. "I bet you'd actually be better than Darryl, cause you seem like you have the smarts. Darryl… man. Hombre was a dumbshit."

I swallowed my shame and looked down at my shoes, a worn pair of Walmart sneakers. "I just want to get to Long Beach."

He shrugged. "Have it your way. Twenty now, the rest once you make the transfer." He threw me the bill and snapped his fingers toward the kitchen. "Let them out, Mama."

*   *   *

We pulled up alongside of the bus station. Merlin rested his wrists on the steering wheel. "Look," he said, "don't screw this up for me. I sorta want to start a side business doing this kind of stuff, and I want Beto to know he can trust me."

I glanced at him. He made me sick. It figured he was just using me. "Well then why didn't you just do it? Why'd you put me up to it?" I could feel the extra heaviness of the package in my bag. Knowing I had drugs on me made my body tingle.

He tapped his head with an index finger. "I'm not the one who wanted to go to Long Beach, brainiac."

I opened the car door and got out. "Thanks for the ride," I said tightly.

Merlin leaned over. "Yeah, good luck finding your sister, Jess. Thanks for the TV."

I bought the bus ticket with the money Beto had given me and tried to look as inconspicuous as possible. If someone shot me a suspicious glance I would smile real friendly like, as if I was just some kid taking the bus to Disneyland. Not someone's mule.

There was a café selling food. I ordered a Coke and two bean burritos and wolfed them down so quickly I hardly tasted them. They announced that my bus was leaving so I headed outside, walked through exhaust and smog, and climbed aboard.

Five

mule (n): a carrier of things.

The bus was almost completely full. People of every color and size sat hunched in their seats, all with the tired, resigned look of those who didn't own cars. I sized up the few empty seats toward the front. There was a spot next to a fat grandma in curlers and another next to a guy in military fatigues. *Nope and double nope.* I cruised toward the back, holding my breath.

In the second-to-last seat was a young guy with a bright-orange Mohawk.

"Can I sit here?" I asked.

He glanced up from texting. "Go ahead." I slumped next to him. He looked me over. "Thank God you're normal." He lifted an eyebrow. "Did you see that guy with the dreads? There are some frickin *crazies* on this bus."

I laughed. "Totally." I took out the sweatshirt I managed to pack and put it on, pulling the hood over my head. The package peeked out from the opened zipper, so I stuffed it down and closed the backpack.

"I'm Karat." His fingernails were painted black, and he had a million earrings going up and down his lobes. He held out his knuckles.

"Jesse." I bumped them. "Carrot?"

"Not the vegetable." He pointed to his head and ears. "K-A-R-A-T. Karat, in like, gold. Get it? It's a play on words. My stage name. Like Macklemore or P!nk. One word. Cool, huh?"

"Cool."

"Yup." He stretched. "On my way to Hollywood. Gettin' ready for my big break." He leaned closer. "I'm a dancer. And a rapper. You want to see something?" He pulled out a flash drive from his pocket. "This is it, baby. My demo tracks. Complete star maker, right here." He flicked the case with his fingernails. On the front was scribbled in black sharpie: KARAT'S KOOL TOONES.

"Wow."

The guy's pupils were enormous, like black eight-balls. And by the way he was talking, all fast and manic, I could tell he was on glass. Great. Of all the empty seats on the bus, I had to go and pick the one next to the tweaker.

I sighed and clutched my backpack tighter to my chest.

"Yeah, I got this friend, he dances with Timberlake. As in, *Justin Timberlake*, can you frickin handle that? So they need another dancer for his upcoming tour, and my friend mentions me, and Justin says, like, cool, get him here, and my friend says, hey, he sings too, and Justin says, dude, have him bring his demo, maybe I can use him in my act." He leaned back in his seat. "Awesome stuff. My friend's gonna pick me up from the bus station."

"Your friend has a car?"

"Sure, sure."

I bit my thumbnail. "Do you think that he could give me a lift to Long Beach?" The bus wasn't getting into Los Angeles until after midnight, and I didn't want to have to call Darla that late. I didn't really want to spend the night in the bus station, either.

He just looked at me.

I shrugged. "I could...pay him something."

He glanced at my backpack. "You have cash?"

Crap. "Well, yeah. A little."

He thought for a moment and then clapped me on the back. "I like you, kid. We'll see what we can do."

He went off about almost making it on American Idol. Man, he wouldn't shut up. I pulled the hood over my head and closed my eyes, hoping he'd catch the hint. Finally, the bus started to pull away.

God, I was tired. Every bone in my body begged for sleep. The engine vibrated through the floor. Within minutes, the motion of the wheels put me out.

*   *   *

I'm surrounded by people. Pony stands on stage singing next to Justin Timberlake. The song ends, and the crowd rushes forward, knocking her to the ground. "Jesse!" she cries. I try to push my way through the crowd, but all the hands, legs, and bodies of the people hold me back. "Pony!" I scream, as I'm dragged to the floor. "Pony...!"

*   *   *

"Hey." I felt someone shaking me awake. I opened an eye to see the lady who sat behind us standing above me. The bus was stopped. It was finally dark outside, and most of the seats were empty. She held her baby in her arms and moved toward the front. "It's a ten-minute bathroom break," she called. "There aren't many places to stop through the Grapevine. Your friend already left."

I felt a breeze blow from the windows through my sweatshirt. Something didn't feel right. I patted down my body. The backpack was gone. Sweat beaded my forehead.

I jumped up and looked under the seats. Nothing. "Holy crap!" The aisle was empty. "Oh my God, oh my God," I cried, checking and double-checking every row. "Shit!"

"Language, please." The bus driver glared up from his magazine.

"My backpack's gone," I said, running up to him. I could barely breathe. "I think the guy next to me lifted it. You know, the guy with the orange Mohawk?"

He shrugged. "Check outside."

I raced off the bus. There was no sign of Karat. I ran to the bathrooms, where most of the people were going. "Hey," I shouted to a group walking back toward the bus, "Did anyone see the orange Mohawk guy? He stole my backpack!"

Most people shook their heads. One guy pointed behind him. "I think I saw him over by the picnic benches."

I ran over. The picnic area was completely empty. My mind whirled in a thousand directions. I had to be dreaming. *This is not real, this can't be real. God, please, make me wake up.* I ran back over to the bus. The army guy leaned against the bus, smoking a cigarette. "Hey," I said, "did you see a guy anywhere with an orange Mohawk?"

His head snapped up. "That strange street kid?" He gave me the once over as if he thought the same thing about me. "I saw him running that way." He shook his head. "Weirdo."

"Thanks." I darted in the direction he showed me, along the freeway toward LA.

"Kid," he called. "The bus will leave without you. You better get back on."

I was sprinting. "Tell him to wait!"

I ran alongside the freeway. Cars zoomed through the darkness, the heat from the gasoline-soaked asphalt blowing against me in waves. I knew Karat rifled through my backpack, and now he was hitchhiking with the jackpot of drugs. Probably enough to finance his whole fake music career. My only chance was to catch him, take the backpack, and kick his ass while I was at it.

I kept running, but there was no sign of him. No, I thought, I'm not losing hope.

Minutes later, the bus—my bus—flew past me, a blast of steamy air blowing my face.

"Stop!" I shouted, waving my arms frantically. "Stop!"

The bus disappeared.

I crumpled to the asphalt and felt my knees hit the ground.

I was completely screwed.

Six

curandero (Spanish): faith healer.

There is stupid and there is *stupid*. As I walked down highway 99, I knew I was one or the other.

You are stupid, Jesse Sampson.

I craned my neck and watched the bus finally disappear over the mountain overpass.

Stupid. I kicked a rock.

Beto's drugs were gone. Actually, I forced myself to remember, they were stolen right from under my nose by a guy with an IQ probably less than even Darryl's. Man, I couldn't even think about the real, serious shit I had managed to get myself in. When Beto found out that I didn't make the transfer, he'd kill me. Or worse.

I walked on the side of the highway with my thumb jerked out. A green sign loomed up ahead. Los Angeles, 125 miles. Dang, 125 miles is a long way. Maybe I'd get lucky and someone would pick me up.

After twenty minutes, the Grapevine didn't look any closer.

I passed by a broken-down minivan with a dad and two kids inside. He was on his cell phone, and they were strapped in their car seats, asleep. My head throbbed. I kept it down, watching my feet as they moved one in front of the other. One two, one two, one two. Every step a little closer.

A CHP motorcycle zoomed past. I hunched my shoulders over and willed myself invisible.

Dontstoppleaseohgoddontstopdontstop.

He pulled over to the side and whirled his lights once.

I sucked in my breath. *Stay smart, Jesse.*

He waited until I walked up to him and stepped off of his bike. "Where're ya going, son?" He had the build of a former high school football player and acne scars to match. "What's your name?"

I glanced behind me. A kernel of hope took root.

"Jay, sir. Jay Smith. My dad and sisters and I are on our way to Los Angeles. Grandma's sick." I shook my head sorrowfully. "Cancer."

I could see the confusion behind his eyes. "Dad?"

"Yeah." I shrugged. "Back there, see? We're the minivan—the silver one." Thank God it was still there, on the side of the road.

"Well, what are you doing here?"

My heart beat hard. "My dad's cell phone's not working. I was going for help."

He turned back to look. "I can call assistance for him."

Sweet Jesus, he was buying it.

"I just hope we can make it there tonight—before it's too late."

He frowned. "I'll go check up on them. I can't put you on my bike, so you'll have to walk back yourself."

I stood up straighter, doing my best Boy Scout impression. "No problem, officer. I'll be right there."

He nodded once, got back on his bike, and headed for the minivan.

I turned in to the field and ran.

∗   ∗   ∗

I didn't dare look back.

Instead, I ran until my lungs burned, clods of dirt churning up in my face. I had almost cleared the field, when I spotted a lone grove of eucalyptus trees clustered by the side of a country road.

Faintly, I heard the dull roar of the freeway deep in the distance. The possibility of the cop coming and looking for me scared me to death. I huddled up against one of the trees and pulled clumpfuls of dead leaves and branches on top until I was fully covered.

It was the second night in a row that I had to sleep outdoors. I stared up at the stars. They twinkled, just like they did back home. For some reason, that made me feel better. In two short days my life had been ripped apart, but at least there were still stars in the sky.

∗   ∗   ∗

A sharp digging in my side awakened me.

"*Mira!*" a voice called. "*El no es muerto.*"

I slit open my eyes and saw yellow cowboy boots inches from my head. I groaned and pushed myself up.

It was barely dawn.

"No, I'm not dead." I knew some Spanish, enough to get the gist of things.

"*Borracho.*" Another voice said this. Soft, feathered laughter peppered the air.

"I'm not drunk, either." I wiped my eyes and tried to focus on the two men facing me, not sure whether to be scared or relieved. "Just lost."

They looked Mexican, with high cheekbones, and weather-beaten faces. "Lost?" repeated the one who kicked me. He narrowed his eyes.

"Uh, no casa," I said, trying to remember my Spanish. "No… madre. No padre."

The older guy nodded his head in sympathy. Now that I was sitting up, I saw that he was positively ancient. He crouched over a small fire, stirred something in a pot, and stared straight ahead, his eyes a milky blue. Blind.

"*Tienes hambre?*" he asked, holding up a spoon.

"*Abuelo,*" said the younger one sharply. "*No. Cuidado.*"

His words should have stung but I was too desperate to care. "Uh, sure," I said, eyeing the pot. My stomach churned at the smell of food. "Yeah."

"*Bueno.*" Abuelo motioned me forward. "*Come, por favor.*"

The younger guy frowned and leaned against a tree trunk, lighting a smoke. It was pretty obvious he didn't trust me too much. I took Abuelo's bowl of rice and beans and ate it in three bites.

"Muy, muy bueno," I said, scraping the empty bowl to get every last grain of rice. It was the best beans and rice I'd ever tasted. "Gracías."

Abuelo chuckled and ladled me some more. He handed me a cup of bitter coffee, which I downed in one gulp. It was intoxicating, how good it felt to have something warm in my stomach, and I wished I could crawl away somewhere and sleep. But gnawing deep inside of me was the sickening memory of the missing backpack, the knowledge of what I'd done. Darla would know what to do, maybe. And Pony—I had to see her, make sure she was okay. I had to get there.

Sleeping bags were crumpled on the other edge of the grove and I spotted a glimpse of a rusted truck with a hatchback tucked behind the trees. A truck.

Maybe, just maybe…

"My name is Jesse." I smiled, hoping it looked friendly enough. "Where are you guys going?"

"Jes-se. *Mucho gusto. Soyel Abuelo, este es Miguelito.*" Abuelo grinned, exposing his last remaining teeth, and pointed at the younger one. "*San Diego.* We go."

"Can I catch a ride?"

Miguelito exhaled a thin stream of smoke. "No," he said, shaking his head. "No room."

I spoke quickly. "I'm just headed to Long Beach. It's right on the way. I'm not too big, I'll just squeeze in—"

"No." This time he walked over to the fire and kicked ashes on top of the last few sputtering embers of the fire. "*Abuelo, vámonos. Es tiempo.*" He glanced sideways as he began gathering the dishes, and I saw the fear in his eyes.

I looked down at myself, with my clothes still covered in dirt and eucalyptus leaves.

He was afraid of me. Who could blame him?

I stood up, the lump hard in my throat. "Well, thanks anyway. Thanks for the food."

Miguelito nodded dismissively and began rolling up the sleeping bags. "*Adíos*," he said.

I walked in the direction of the freeway. The sun had already cleared the mountains and the promise of its heat pulsed down on the field. It would be a long walk, I knew.

"*Muchacho, espera.*" Abuelo cleared his throat and whispered something to his grandson. "*Espera.*"

I stopped walking and turned around. "What?"

"*Tus manos.*"

I shrugged my shoulders in exasperation and slapped my hands against my sides. "My *what*?"

Miguelito spoke up. "Your *hands*," he said, rolling his eyes. "He wants to see your hands."

Nice to know he spoke English this whole time, I thought with annoyance. "What for?"

He stepped forward with a grudging expression. "*Abuelo* is a *curandero*. A faith healer. He can read people. He wants to see who you are."

I looked at my hands, caked with mud. The hands that throttled Merlin. The hands that took the drugs. The hands that hid Pony and helped me escape.

"Do I have to?"

"Only if you want a ride."

I hesitated. A ride would get me there in two hours.

"Jes-se." Abuelo just smiled and pointed to me. "*Sientese.*"

For some reason, I listened. I guess I figured that I had nothing to lose at that point, since I already was walking and had no pride left to speak of. I walked back over to where Abuelo sat and crouched down beside him. He reached over and took my right hand in his, closing his eyes and lifting his face to the sky. He hummed a little, under his breath.

"Well?" I asked, when I could stand it no longer. "What do you see?"

"*Sí*," he said. He opened those unseeing eyes and stared right at me, through me. "He is Jesse." He slapped my cheeks and grinned. "Okay. Long Beach. We take him there."

Seven

pervert (n): one given to some form of sexual perversion.

I sat in the hatchback with Abuelo as the truck groaned up the grade. It was filled floor to ceiling with crates stamped *Washington Apples*.

Miguelito wasn't lying when he said there was no room. Abuelo was wedged in the corner, and he snored softly against his pillow. I leaned against the wooden crates and watched the landscape of craggy mountains pass through the sliver of window.

After a couple hours, the truck pulled off the exit that said Long Beach. We drove to a gas station and stopped. Abuelo woke up with a snort and scratched his head.

"Hey." I patted him on the leg. "This is my stop here. I just wanted to say thanks. For the ride."

He grunted and nodded.

I opened the hatch and rested my hand against the door. "...

Abuelo? You can really read people?"

He nodded. "*Sí.*"

"And you…read me?" I felt my cheeks redden when I said this.

This time he leaned forward. "Sí, Jes-se." Despite his lined face and opaque eyes, an energy crackled about him that you couldn't see, but feel. It gave me the chills.

He knew. I could sense it. *He knew everything.*

"What did you see?" I whispered. "When you read my hand? Will I find her? Will I get back home?"

He smiled. "*Sigue buscando,*" he said in a soft, gravelly voice.

"Sigue…what?" I laughed lightly, trying to break the heaviness I felt in the air. "Looking? Are you saying that I should keep looking?"

He nodded again, and closed his eyes.

Keep looking. That's what I was doing, wasn't it?

Crazy old man, I told myself. I was crazy, too, because for a second there I actually believed all that stuff.

"Later, Abuelo," I said. He was already back to snoring, his mouth slightly opened.

I climbed out of the truck and walked away.

*   *   *

The guy who worked in the Chevron minimart said that Aunt Darla's address was only four miles away. Four miles I could do. Despite my thighs, which were chafed raw from sleeping in my jeans, I walked with a little bounce to my step because I was so happy.

I was almost there.

I walked through neighborhoods until I began to hit the rougher part of town. I figured that Aunt Darla would have wanted to live closer to school, but it was probably cheaper to rent around here. Her apartment complex was a gray series of buildings named Sandy Shores. The H was gone from the name so really it looked like Sandy *Sores.* Merlin would have had something moronic to say about that. I climbed the rusty stairs and knocked on her door.

After a while, it finally opened. My aunt's head poked out of the narrow crack. "Can I help you?"

"Aunt Darla, it's me, Jesse." I brushed the hair out of my eyes and smiled.

"Oh, my God." She opened the door a tiny bit more and squinted at me. "Jesse. I didn't recognize—is that really you?"

My mouth tugged. "Yeah. I guess I grew a lot since the last time you saw me." After all, I was only like eleven, and she was just a teenager. She had gotten older, too. A Led Zeppelin tank top stretched across her chest and yesterday's eyeliner smudged down below her eyes.

She stepped back from the door and motioned me inside. The apartment was completely darkened, the blinds drawn with blankets over them for good measure. It had a dank, musty smell and I wondered if she had been sick. She slumped down at the kitchen table.

"Is everything okay?"

"Yeah." She rubbed her eyes and yawned. "Just tired." It was already past noon.

I noticed that the bedroom door was closed.

"So, where's Pony?"

She pulled her tangled hair off her face and let it fall behind her shoulders. "God. Jesse, you should have called me. I tried you back on your mom's number."

Only she was arrested, and Darla knew that. Plus Mom's phone had no more minutes, anyway. "Called you? I did call you. Remember? You told me to find a way here."

"Yeah." Her mouth turned downward. "That was before."

"Aunt Darla," I said, feeling my pulse quicken. "Where's Pony?" I looked at the closed door.

She glanced down at her chipped nail polish. "She's not here."

Pony's not here. She really just said that.

Pony's not here.

Not.

Here.

I wet my lips, trying to remain calm. "Well, where is she?"

"Jesse." She held her forehead with her fingertips. "I don't know, okay? They—they wouldn't let her come here."

"Why?"

She groaned, stood up, and pulled a carton of orange juice from the refrigerator. "I didn't pass clearance."

"What does *that* mean?"

She waved in the direction of the closed bedroom. "My boyfriend, Stan." She tilted the carton and swigged it. "He's got a record."

My face froze. "What kind of record?"

She closed her eyes and splayed out her fingertips, in exasperation. "You know, he's …registered. He can't be around kids."

"Why?" I felt my teeth grit, the blood throb between my ears. "What's the reason he can't he be around kids?"

Say it. Just say it.

I knew the answer, but I wanted to hear it from her, that she chose some slimeball perverted CHILD MOLESTER over my little sister.

She glared up at me. "Look, he got framed, okay? It was his niece—her mother's a real nut case and she put her up to it. Stan would never hurt anyone, he's innocent."

They all are.

I sank into a chair and held my head. "I can't believe it." I came so far, risked my life even, *for nothing.* "This is so incredibly fucked up."

She didn't argue. Instead, she just stared straight ahead. She seemed so zoned out, so indifferent that I wished I could throttle her.

"Hey." She lifted her eyes. "Some guy called for you, here. Merlin or something? That's a weird name."

Shit. I almost forgot about him. I used his phone to call Darla back at the trailer. Of course he'd try to call the number.

Shit. Shit. *Shit.*

"Really? What did he say?"

"He was looking for you, he said. Didn't sound too happy. He wanted you to call him."

This day could not get any worse. Here I was, four hours away from Truckston, no idea where Pony was, with a pothead and probably drug dealer on my tail. And now my aunt, shacking up with some pervert.

The door to the bedroom finally opened. Out walked a guy in his forties with thin hair, a beer belly, and the biggest lips I'd ever seen on a white guy. Yeah, the dude had perv written all over his face. "Maybe you could talk *louder* out here," he snapped. He stomped to the bathroom.

I shot Darla a look.

"He's good to me," she sniffed. We could hear the sound of him peeing through the door. "He loves me."

"You chose *him* over my little sister?" I said it in a low voice.

"Look, you ungrateful snot, I haven't even seen you guys in years, then you show up on my doorstep giving me shit about Pony. Last time I saw her, she was a baby. I have my own life to live, you know. Damn, it's just like Annette to go and assume I'm going to raise her kids when she gets her ass thrown in jail."

"She doesn't even know."

Because of course, she was in jail. Sobering up and bawling or finding Jesus or worrying about us or not giving a shit—it didn't matter because she wasn't here, being a mom. But then, she hasn't been one for a long time.

Darla scratched at the sores on her face. What in *the hell* happened to Darla going to college? *Her job?*

Pedophile Stan got out of the bathroom and began making himself an omelet. He didn't say hello or offer me one.

"I want to take a shower," I said, giving Darla the eye. "And eat something."

Darla looked at me and nodded. I thought I could see a hint of guilt.

"Sure. Okay, Jesse." She pointed to the bathroom, and I went inside, slamming the door behind me.

Eight

```
nightmare (n): a dream producing a feeling of
              anxiety or terror.
```

I let the entire bathroom steam up. I stood with the hot water pouring off of me and scrubbed every inch of my body until each of my fingers was shriveled like Abuelo's. I didn't care if Darla was mad for wasting her hot water.

She owed me.

My clothes were so filthy that I washed them out in the sink and hung them up to dry. I grabbed a towel from the ground and tied it around my waist.

When I got back out, Darla was camped out in front of the TV, flipping through the channels.

"Where's your boyfriend?" I asked, with a little edge.

She rolled her eyes. "He went to work. But look, I found you an extra T-shirt." She handed me a wrinkled Dodgers tee. "And these shorts." I held them out gingerly. "Don't worry," she smirked.

"They're not Stan's."

I put on the shorts, praying to God there wasn't anything communicable growing in them. Maybe she was trying to be decent, but I wasn't letting her off so easy. "I need to figure out what I'm going to do," I said, pulling on the T-shirt. "Can I crash here for a couple of days?"

She paused on an episode of Jerry Springer. "Just as long as Stan's probation officer doesn't catch wind of it."

Empty beer cans and cigarette butts littered the coffee table. I sat down next to her on the stained couch.

"What happened when the social workers came? Did you get a number for anyone? A name? Anything?"

She rummaged through her purse until she found a business card, which she handed to me. *Geraldine Guerrera, Social Worker II, County of Orange, California.* "She was real nice about it, actually," she said a little softer.

"Did she tell you where Pony is?"

"No." Her eyes were dull as she stared at the screen. "Somewhere in Truckston, I guess. Jesse," she said, her voice cracking, "I really would have done it, you know. Taken you kids in. If things were different."

I looked at her face, deeply etched with lines that didn't belong on someone who was only twenty-one. "I always believed you when you said you'd never turn out like Mom," I said in a quiet voice. "You were going to be a nurse. What happened?"

"Yeah." She gave a short laugh and wiped her eyes. "School was harder than I thought, and I got into some trouble, and then I lost my job…" She clicked the channel again, this time to an infomercial. "But I gotta take care of myself, first. You know?"

"Sure."

But I didn't know, really. Because for as long as I can remember, I have taken care of Pony. Every day, a constant, nagging worry about whether she ate, whether she slept, whether she'd get lice again. When she needed new shoes. When she needed Christmas presents. And now that I didn't even know where she was, that sense of missing her ate away at me like some bad cancer.

I took a deep breath. "I'll figure it out."

Darla left to go somewhere, and I just laid on the couch, crashing hard.

*   *   *

I woke up eight hours later.

My head felt groggy and was filled with lingering images of my dreams. Restless, crazy nightmares about Beto and Pony and Mom. I got up and grabbed a few pieces of stale pizza from the fridge. Though it was finally dark, kids were still playing ball in the street.

It sounded like Darla and Stan were back. Light seeped from under the bedroom door, and I could hear them laughing and giggling. *Sick.* I sunk back into the couch and rubbed my forehead.

I needed to get out of here.

Darla's phone rang.

I picked it up off of the coffee table and glanced at the number. A rush of sweat hit my armpits when I saw that the area code was from Truckston.

What do I do? I felt light-headed as I held the phone in my palm. I didn't recognize the number, but what if it was Pony?

But then, what if it was Merlin?

Maybe I shouldn't answer it.

Maybe I should.

I should.

I flipped it open. "Hello?"

"You motherfucker."

I closed my eyes. "Merle, I can explain."

"I can't even believe you had the nerve to answer your aunt's phone. Do you have any idea what you've done, Jesse? Beto—he's beyond pissed. That shit was worth $2000."

"It got stolen, Merle. You have to believe me. On the bus, there was this wasted guy—"

"See? Words, all fucking words. I don't believe you, cause, what do you think I am, *stupid*?" His voice thinned into a whine. "How could it get stolen on the frickin bus? God, Jess, all you had to do was just sit there. *Sleep.* Give the dude the damn package and then live your little pathetic life."

"Pony's not here. I got to Darla's, and Merlin, she's gone."

"That's the thing, Jesse. Why I'm calling. Because, I know, and so does Beto."

"What are you talking about?"

"Pony. Your sister's in Truckston."

My heart lurched. "How do you know that?" I whispered.

"Oh, our little friend, Wilma, was looking for you the other day back in the 'hood. She's a real nice social worker, that Wilma, and I may have happened to mention that I knew where you were." He sneered. "And Wilma, her dress was real pretty, and I told her so, and she just happened to let it slip…"

"You're full of shit. She wouldn't have told you anything. God,

Merlin, quit messing with me. What's the matter with you? You're freaking me out."

"Beto knows Pony's here somewhere. And he wants his product back, or at least what it's worth. Two thousand big ones."

"I don't have it. I told you, it wasn't my fault. I'm not lying." I tried to stop my voice from shaking. "I just need some time, but I'll get him the money back, Merlin. Swear."

"Look, I don't really give a shit. All I know is, you screwed your old buddy Merlin out of a good thing he had coming, and little girls, man…" His voice trailed off as he inhaled. "Sometimes bad things happen to little girls."

"Don't you dare touch her." My hands turned to ice. "I will rip you to shreds if you so much as hurt one hair on her head."

"You heard what I said, bro. The money or Pony."

The line went dead.

Nine

thief (n): one who steals especially stealthily
                    or secretly.

Every time I dialed his phone it went to message. Yet I sat there in the shadows, punching in the numbers again and again.

I tore my fingers through my hair. *They knew where she was. They threatened*—I shook my head, feeling sick. They threatened to hurt her.

What had I done?

I had to go back, and as soon as possible. I had to explain to Beto what really happened, and then start paying him back what I owed him. Whatever it took. I'd work the whole summer, maybe get a job working in the fields, oh God, whatever it took.

I looked around the empty apartment and heard a giggle through the wall. I knew Darla couldn't help me, and I couldn't tell her.

That's when I noticed it.

A fat wallet, resting on the top of the TV.

Stan's, probably.

I jiggled my knee up and down, up and down. Wiped my nose and hugged my chest.

I'll just look.

There's no harm in looking. People do it all the time. It's curiosity, for God's sake. I got up from the couch and walked over to the TV. I reached over and grabbed the wallet. Opened it up.

His driver's license, taken back when he had more hair. A Starbucks card. Costco card. His pictures—Stan with a middle-aged fat wife and two fat teenage sons, all wearing identical blue shirts and standing in front of a Christmas tree. That pissed me off. *Nice, Stan, real nice. Does wifey know what you do with Darla in your spare time? I mean, besides the child molesting?*

Behind the picture was an employee identification card for some computer company. Wedged down beneath the leather, was a thin gold band. So he took off his wedding ring before he screwed my aunt. How classy.

I waited until the very end to look into the billfold. Slowly I opened it up and saw layers of green. *Oh, yes.* Twenties.

I'd never stolen before. I wasn't a thief. Well, only that one time when Pony was a baby and Mom started using again.

At first, she tried to stay clean, she was so proud of her pretty baby girl that she promised to give us the world. "I'm going back to school, Jess," she said. "Make something of myself. I always got A's in English. We'll live in a real house, with a yard."

I could build a tower with those dreams. But then, Darryl and her made up and soon, she was gone again on the weekends.

The first time it happened, I woke up in the middle of the night with Pony crying beside me. She sounded like a bleating lamb, over and over again. She was probably starving, that much I knew, only we didn't have any more formula. So, at eleven at night, I left Pony in her crib, and ran down to the minimart. Slunk in while the cashier had his back turned watching the TV. Took a can of formula and slunk back out.

I was ten.

The bills felt crisp against the pad of my thumb. If I took a few, he'd probably not even notice.

I'm not a bad guy.

Pony.

For Pony.

I took four bills, grabbed my backpack, and ran out of the apartment.

*   *   *

I jogged down the darkened streets, toward the bus terminal I passed on my way to Darla's. The money bounced in my pocket. Really, I only took about enough to buy a ticket and a little extra to eat. I'd call Darla later, explain. She'd understand. She'd have to.

A thick marine layer covered the sky. Loud, thumping music poured from every open window and car that passed by. Since school was just over, the streets were alive with kids yelling and screaming and partying. Girls in low-cut tops hung out of car windows and shouted at me as they drove by. I kept my head down and tried to remain invisible. Just a few more blocks.

A group of black kids were clustered on a street corner.

Someone had his iPod on, and the music pulsed into the air. I tried to swerve around them when I bumped against someone's shoulder. Out of the corner of my eye I saw a girl skid into one of her friends and fall down.

Shit.

Her friend in a purple mini dress helped her up. I slowed and wheeled back around. "Sorry. I'm sorry," I said, offering her my hand.

But it was too late. The crowd already turned to face me. The girl, in tight jeans and a sequined top, brushed herself off and glared at me.

I swallowed. "It was an accident."

"Hold up," said a guy standing next to her with gold earrings. "Where are you from, white boy?" He blocked my path. The entire group watched.

"Uh." I sized up the crowd. They had the buzzed, excited faces of people looking for action. "Out of town." I took a step back.

"Don't you know? You're in the wrong neighborhood," he said, bumping my chest with his. "You stupid or what?"

I could see the bus station up ahead on the corner of the next block. It was so close. I didn't have time for this bullshit. "Yeah, man, I guess I'm stupid." I tried to push past him.

He grabbed my shirt. "Will you look at that? This clown's trying to disrespect me," he said to his buddies. A few murmured in agreement.

"No, I'm not."

"I think you need to get taught a lesson." He twisted the collar of my tee in his fist. "Need to give us some type of payment."

Sweat slid down my back. "No, look, I'm sorry. I just need to get to the bus sto—"

"Damien," he tilted his head toward the big guy behind him, "Search him."

"No!" I twisted away and flung myself toward the street. I just had to make it across.

"Get him!"

The heavy thud of the crowd's footsteps followed me. The shine from brake lights and storefronts blinded my eyes. I was halfway into the street when I felt hands around my neck, pulling me to the ground.

"Get off me!" I writhed as they held me down and searched my pockets. Car horns blared. I heard the crunch of the bills as they pulled them out.

"Dude's frickin loaded!" shouted the one called Damien. Those were his hands around my neck, and I twisted my face to his arm, biting hard. He cuffed me in the jaw. "Motherfucker bit me!"

"I'll teach you how it goes down around here." Gold earring guy held me up by the hair and punched me hard in the gut.

Firecrackers exploded behind my eyes.

I crumpled into a fetal position on the asphalt.

"Give me my money," I groaned.

The group had me circled. Someone kicked my head. I bit my tongue and tasted blood. Gold earring guy was holding me by the hair again when I heard the single whirl of a siren. A police car screeched right in front of us. Through slitted eyes I saw two officers get out.

"Cops!" someone yelled. "Clear out."

The group fled.

I struggled to hold my body up by my arms.

"That guy took my money."

Stan's stolen money, of course, but it was the only thing I had. Not even the clothes I wore were mine.

The second officer ran after the group. The first one stood over me and whipped out his flashlight. He shone it into my eyes. "I need to see some identification," he said. "And I'm going to ask you to get up and answer a few questions."

I scrambled up and held my stomach. My head spun but I forced myself to stand, swaying slightly. "I'm Jesse. Jesse Sampson," I said, struggling to breathe. "From Truckston." I bent over and spat blood on the asphalt. "I'm a runaway."

I just couldn't run anymore.

Ten

Emerson Children's Hall (n): a Los Angeles County Emergency Shelter housing nondelinquent neglected and sexually, physically, or emotionally abused children ranging in ages from 0-17. The Hall provides shelter to about 4000 children annually on a temporary basis.

It was well past midnight when we pulled up in front of a huge, three-story building surrounded by a tall iron fence with spikes on the top. I sat up a little and rubbed my eyes.

"Is this Social Services?"

The police officer met my gaze in the rear-view mirror. "Not exactly."

Past the front of the building stretched a chain-link fence topped with barbed wire. Beyond the fence were clusters of buildings lit up with floodlights.

The hairs on my neck rose up into a little forest. "Are you

putting me in juvie?"

"No," he said. "Step out of the car, please."

Some guy was waiting for us at the gate and buzzed us in. He was bald with a goatee and wore a badge around his neck. He looked at me and yawned.

If this wasn't juvie, then I sure as hell wanted to know what it was, because it sorta seemed like a place they didn't want people leaving.

"Good luck," called the police officer before he stepped back into his car.

"I'm Gary," said the bald guy. "Come with me. We'll get you processed." He put a hand on my shoulder and led me toward the building.

Processed?

"What is this place?"

"Emerson Children's Hall. Your first time?"

"Am I in trouble or something?" Maybe Stan had already called to report that his money was missing. Maybe they found Beto's drugs and got my fingerprints off of it. I could be completely screwed.

He gave a short laugh. "No. This is an emergency shelter. Like foster care. Have you been in foster care before?"

I clenched my jaw. "It's been a while."

We went inside a darkened reception area and passed a security officer leaning against the wall. Gary led me down a long hallway until we reached the one room with a fluorescent light on.

A woman with blue scrubs on sat typing at a computer. She assessed me with narrowed eyes.

"Well. According to Officer Denton, you are Jesse Sampson.

Is that correct?"

"Yeah."

"I'm LaVonda," she said. "I pulled up your file. You're considered missing in your county. Truckston, huh? You've managed to come a long way."

"Maybe."

She looked at me coolly. "So you think you're a tough guy. Was that fight you were in connected with any gang? That won't go over well, here."

"I'm not in any gang." I craned my neck toward the monitor. I could see the words *Annette Sampson* and my own name. "Does that thing tell you where my sister is? She was supposed to be with my aunt."

She pushed a button on the keyboard, causing the screen to go blank, and spun around on her chair. "You'll get to talk to a social worker eventually. She can answer those questions for you."

Gary pointed to a small room with an examination table. "Please takeoff your clothing in here. We need to search you."

"Search?" Those little hairs rose up again when I heard that. "I don't need to be searched."

Now LaVonda stood up. "It's just procedure, son. Safety regs. You have to understand, kids have been knifed here, before. We need to take any personal belongings you have as well."

I felt the room grow smaller. "I don't have any."

"Let's go," Gary said. He pushed me in the direction of the room.

My body tensed. "Look, I'm not even supposed to be here," I said, my voice raising. "I need to be back in Truckston, with my sister. Can't someone just take me there in the morning?"

The security officer appeared in the doorway. LaVonda faced me. "I *said*, the social worker will answer all those questions for you. *Later.* For now, we need to get you processed and into bed, so please step inside the examination room and remove your clothing."

My knees felt like jelly. I felt beads of sweat pop out on my forehead. "No fucking way. Nobody's touching me."

LaVonda looked past me. "Gary?" she said in a calm, bitchy voice. "Looks like this is going to be a Code 5."

I felt two hands grip my forearms. "Procedure, son." Gary was surprisingly strong as he pushed me into the examination room.

At that moment, I decided that no one was touching me. Something inside me snapped. "Get the fuck off of me!" I thrashed against his grip like some kind of animal.

The security guard held me down by the neck, and Gary pushed me to the ground. I tensed against him and kicked the wall behind me.

"Remain still," Gary shouted. "Remain still!" The tile was cold and cut into my cheekbone.

"No!" I writhed and turned and strained against them. All I could think about was Pony, and how I couldn't get myself trapped here. It felt like my anger was exploding through my skin.

Only it didn't make me feel better, only worse.

In the end, they won.

*   *   *

Gary and the security guard escorted me down the darkened hallway. We left the main building and walked over to the cluster of barrack-style buildings. "This is your cottage," said Gary. "Senior Boys.

No more funny business, Jesse Sampson. You don't want to spend your first night in solitary."

I kept my mouth shut. So this place wasn't juvie but they have solitary confinement. Nice. We walked into one of the buildings and were greeted by another guy wearing a badge that said *Staff*.

"This one's a fighter," Gary said to the guy.

I shot him a look that told him what I thought of him.

They led me into a darkened room. It looked like a large TV room, with several vinyl couches. Connected to the TV room were what looked like dormitory-style bedrooms, with rows of beds. He led me inside one of the rooms and pointed to an empty cot.

"That's yours. There a toothbrush on top and your clothes for tomorrow. You have five minutes to go do your necessaries and get under those covers."

The guy in the bed by the door sat up and groaned. He squinted at me.

"Aw, shit," he said, punching his pillow. "Not another white kid."

"Zip it, Tomas." Gary kicked the leg of his bed.

I crawled into bed. My stomach and lip throbbed from the fight back in Long Beach. Pain radiated out from my jaw where I'd been kicked. But worse still was the humiliation I felt from being restrained and searched. I couldn't stop my body from shaking.

"You're new," a voice next to me whispered. "First time?"

I rolled over to the other side with my back to him. This wasn't day-care. I wasn't about to start making friends in the middle of the night.

"Don't worry," said the voice to my back. "You'll get used to this place."

Like hell I would.

Eleven

enemy (n): one who is antagonistic to another.

An alarm woke us up at seven. About forty guys slept in my cottage, and we were roughly all around the same age. A few smiled, but most of them just looked, sizing me up. We dressed quickly, showered, and were herded down the hallway toward the cafeteria.

The kid who slept next to me the night before shadowed me like a dog.

When he stepped on the backs of my sneakers for the second time, I turned around. "You got a problem?" I asked. "Why are you walking so close to me?"

He was skinny—skinnier than even me, and short, with wild, wide-spaced eyes. "Oh, sorry—but you see, Gary—he told me I had to show you around, help you, since you're new and all."

"I think I can figure things out," I said, walking inside the cafeteria. The place was full of kids, and it could have been any school cafeteria, except for the fact that everyone wore the same thing: white T-shirts that said Emerson Hall in block lettering and dark, cheap-looking jeans. Two security guards stood at each entrance with blank looks on their faces.

"Well, if you do," he said with a laugh, "let me know, 'cause I'll never be able to figure this place out."

I looked him over. The kid seemed to be in constant motion, twitching and bouncing on the balls of his feet. He began rubbing his hands up and down the whitened scars that ran the length of his arms. "What's your name?" I asked.

"Timemmett."

We got in line. I grabbed my tray and was handed a juice by a hair-netted worker.

"Tim—*what*?"

"Tim Emmett. Sorry, I just talk fast—I can't help it, I have ADHD. You're Jesse, I already know. Resisted examination—real ballsy move, trying that right off the bat."

I stared, openmouthed. "How do you know that?"

"Trust me, after a while, you'll know everything about this place, too."

*   *   *

Over pancakes and eggs, Tim Emmett gave me the low-down,. After talking to him, I decided that there was virtually nothing that he didn't know.

"There's around three hundred kids living here," he said, swigging his milk. "It's like a big holding house for when they can't find a kid a foster home. Emergency shelter. From babies all the way to seventeen. The little kids go into foster care pretty quick, unless they're mental. I heard there was this five-year-old here for a year because he killed all the cats in his foster home." He took a stab at his pancakes and then pushed his plate away, grimacing. "Nasty. These things are like eating rubber."

I hardly looked up at him; I was shoveling in the food so fast. It was the best meal I'd had in weeks. I took a whole sausage and crammed it in my mouth.

"—But the older kids, we tend to stay at the Hall longer. Some never leave." Apparently Tim Emmett was a talker. The kid hardly took a breath between sentences.

"How long have you been in here?"

"This time?" He wrinkled his nose, thinking. "Five months, I think. I'm on the waiting list for a group home in Montana for kids like me."

I eyed his hardly touched plate. "Kids like you?"

"Yeah, I'm a pyro," he said cheerfully. "I cut sometimes, too. And I sniff paint. Plus whatever other shit I can get my hands on. Ha. I've been in like, twenty foster homes." He puffed out his chest. "It's almost a record around here, except for Tomas, of course. He's been in more. Juvie, too." He noticed me drooling at his food. "You want this? Go for it. I don't eat too much. It's my meds."

I grabbed his plate and dug in. "Who's Tomas? Him?" I motioned toward an enormous kid who sat apart from the others, hunched over his breakfast.

"Nah. That's the Indian. But stay away from him, too. People say he's dangerous."

"Dangerous?" I studied the Indian. He had high cheekbones

and deep-set eyes, and the width of his shoulders seemed about twice the size of mine. But his expression was what stopped me—it was without any emotion, just pure stone. Yeah, I guess dangerous I could buy. "Why?"

Tim shook his head. "Keeps to himself. Won't talk, really, like to anyone. But, that's how it is around here. Psychos, delinquents, perverts—crazy kids everywhere. Look over there," he said in a low voice. "Tomas is that guy down at the end."

He pointed to a tough-looking Hispanic guy with a shaved head and tattooed lettering across his forehead. He was surrounded by half of the boys in the cottage.

He was the one who popped off when I came in last night. All during breakfast, I caught him glaring at me.

"What's his deal?"

He shrugged. "His brother's a big-time gang leader in East LA. Doing hard time for killing two guys. Guess he's trying to live up to his rep. Just a warning: Tomas always messes with the new guys. I think it's because he's ODD."

"ADHD, ODD—are those all shrink words or something?"

"Oppositional defiant disorder. Except, come to think about it, that's every frickin' kid in here, just about. Yeah." He gave a short laugh. "With all the therapy I've had in here, I could have myself a degree in psy-*call*-logy."

I looked down at the table. Sure enough, Tomas was giving me a laser beam stare, like issuing a challenge. I lifted my chin and met his gaze.

Tim Emmett watched. "*Shit*," he breathed. "What are you doing? Don't look at him! You gotta be careful. You don't want to go picking a fight with Tomas if you don't have to. He's the king psycho of all psychos—plus he never fights fair."

"Really?" I said under my breath. "Bring it on."

Before my freak-out with Merlin, I had only gotten in a couple fights at school. Now it seemed I was averaging one a day. The thought of hitting another person with my fist sounded good. Real good. I set my jaw and continued to stare. After about ten seconds, Tomas looked away.

Point one, Jesse. I gave him the tiniest smile.

I looked into my cup of orange juice and swirled it around and around. My stomach felt pleasantly full for the first time in weeks. I wondered if Pony was eating better now, wherever she was.

The thought of her made my heart lurch.

"Are there any social workers around here?" I asked.

I needed to go back to Truckston, the sooner the better.

He laughed. "Are you kidding, man? This place is crawling with them. Around here, they're all social workers."

A group of guys from the other end of the table passed us on Tim's side. Most of them were Mexican, and all had that cocky swagger of being a part of the group. Tomas walked right behind Tim, and without warning, smacked him in the back of the head. Tim lost his balance and fell off his chair. His arm hit the glass of milk and sent it skidding across. White drops sprayed everywhere.

"What the hell?" I leapt up and clenched my fists.

Tomas laughed, staring straight at me, and righted the empty glass. He helped Tim up and ruffled his hair. "Hey, sorry Tim Em. You just had a *mosquito* on your head. Big, nasty *white* sucker."

Tomas' group laughed behind him as Tim attempted to blot his T-shirt with a napkin. I handed him mine and turned to Tomas. "You're an asshole."

"Oh, really now, *ese*?" Tomas said, his lips curling. "Is that the way white trash country boys talk?"

I sized him up this time. He was shorter than me by about half a foot, but more muscled and compact. But still, I bet I could take him, *vato* homeboys and all. That I was sure of.

I smiled. "Would you rather I called you a *culo . . . ese*?"

One of his homeboys sneered, and Tomas' hand shot out and cuffed him, hard. When he turned to face me, his eyes bulged with fury. "Let's take this outside," he said through gritted teeth.

"Jesse." Tim threw the napkins down and stepped toward me. "Please, just drop it. I'm fine, really." He lifted his arms, which were still sticky with milk. "See?"

Tomas looked from Tim to me. "See, Timmy E knows his place around here, like a good boy. Maybe he just needs to tell you how things run. *Comprende*?"

I was going to show this guy exactly my place around here.

"You know what? I think I can already tell for myself who the dickheads are."

He took a swing at me, and I ducked. That rage, red and throbbing and by now so familiar, buzzed through me, and I jumped up, clearing the table. Plates clattered to the floor. He grabbed my hair, and I socked him in the stomach. We fell together on the cafeteria floor, a tangle of arms, legs, and fists.

"Fight, fight, fight," chanted the cafeteria crowd.

But I could barely hear, my brain was so filled with the desire to feel his bones crunch beneath me.

* * *

I sat in a closed white room with nothing in it but a cot.

Kids' names, all kinds of cuss words, and gang tags were scratched into the peeling paint. The one lone window was small and positioned high, near the ceiling.

I heard angry, rhythmic thumps coming from the other side of the wall. My guess was that Tomas was in the room next to me.

The door creaked opened. In walked a blond guy wearing wire-rimmed glasses and frayed Dockers. In a geeky kind of way, he looked like a surfer, complete with a sunburned nose and white-blonde eyebrows — except for his badge and the clipboard he carried.

"Hi," he said, and stretched out his hand. "We haven't met. I'm Seth."

I crossed my arms and stared at him. After a few beats he let his arm fall and sat down next to me. "Rough day?"

I scoffed.

"You want to talk about it?"

"Look, I get it. You're the shrink."

"Sort of." He smiled. "Actually, I'm an intern—still in school. Not quite a psychologist yet."

"So you're a fake shrink."

He laughed. "I hope not. Maybe more like a student shrink. But let's forget about all that for now, can we do that?" He set the clipboard down next to him. "Do you know why you're here?"

I scanned the dingy white walls and rested my head against the hard concrete blocks. "Like in this room?" I shrugged. "Probably for knocking that gangbanger on his ass back there."

"Tomas. Ah, yes. He can be a troublemaker."

"He got what he deserved."

"Let's talk about you. You've had some anger issues, Jesse. Would that be a fair assumption?" He clicked the pen he carried and tapped the clipboard. "The notes here say the police picked you up during a fight. You resisted the examination. And then now you start a fight on the first day of your—"

"And then *now*?" I lifted my head. "Look, Mr. Psychology, maybe you should write this on your little clipboard there. Four days ago the cops bust into my house, jail my mom, and take my sister. I hitch a ride the whole way here to find her, she was supposed to be with my aunt, and now she's not. I have no idea where she is, but I think she's in trouble. Big trouble. Now I'm in this kid's prison and nobody will even tell me why." The image of reaching under the bed, feeling for her little body and grabbing nothing but dirty clothes flashed before me. I wiped my eyes with my fist. "Yeah, I'd say I have some fucking anger issues. What do you think?"

"Oh." He pressed his lips together and picked up the clipboard again. "I see." The room fell silent. His eyes softened and he cocked his head. "Why do you think your sister is in trouble?"

"I have my reasons."

"What reasons?"

The temptation to spill the whole drug mule thing was on the tip of my tongue, but I knew if I did, I'd probably find my ass in juvie. It was just such a huge burden sitting on top of my chest, knowing that Beto and Merlin were still out there, pissed off about the stolen money. And Merlin — he threatened to hurt Pony. My stomach clenched.

I just felt so goddamn tired. "Just reasons."

"No one's talked to you about your case? Not during intake? Not your social worker?"

"No one."

Seth looked at me for a long time before speaking.

"Jesse," he said. He leaned forward. "I want you to know, I'm on your side, okay? I want to help."

I stared at him, bored to frickin' tears. "Oh, really."

"Look, let me talk to some people, see if I can find out what's going on."

My whole life, adults have made promised to me that they had no plans to keep. My mother. Darryl. Teachers. Social workers. After a while, promises just become words—empty, useless words.

I leaned back. The concrete blocks were cool against my back.

"Whatever you say. You know where I'll be."

But not for long.

Twelve

friend (n): someone who has your back.

They let us out of solitary right after lunch. Gary and another Senior Boys' counselor lined us up, side by side, outside of the administrative offices.

"Stay away from each other," Gary warned, "or else next time we'll call security and it'll be juvie."

"This armpit sucks ass compared to juvie," Tomas shot back, tipping his chin up in defiance. "At least that place isn't filled with *gabachos locos.*" His eyes slid over to mine tauntingly.

Gary's finger hovered inches from his face. "You want to mess with me, Tomas? Huh? Cause I'd be happy to arrange another couple *days* in solitary for you, would you like that? ...*Would* you?" He jabbed him in the cheek.

Tomas didn't even flinch, just stared back at him, his jaw locked into a tight clench. His neck, I now noticed, was covered in a long, stretching tattoo of a skull with flowers in place of eye sockets, and a thin, pink scar cut halfway through it.

"No. No sir," he said, finally.

"Good." Gary smiled, clearly pleased with himself. "What about you, Sampson? Had enough of solitary? Or do you want to start some shit with me, too?"

"No, I'm good," I said, stifling a smile. Just seeing Tomas rattled by Gary was worth it.

Gary, man — dude had the biggest ego trip this side of Hitler.

We were escorted back to Senior Boys' cottage, where it was rec time. Outside it had been humid and I was surprised by the cooler air when I stepped inside. All heads snapped up when they saw us.

Tomas cut in with his posse, who all shot me furtive, challenging glances. I ignored them and went into the sleeping dormitory to lie on my cot. I had a massive headache. During our fight, Tomas had opened up the scab on my fat lip and banged my head up pretty good against the cafeteria floor. A decent-sized goose egg throbbed on the back of my skull. I probed the area gingerly with my fingertips and winced.

"Hey, Jesse." Tim Emmett came and sat down on the cot next to me. "Mind if I sit here?"

"It's your bed. Do what you want."

"Oh. Yeah, huh?" He jiggled his legs and grabbed his pillow, hugging it to his chest as he stared at me. I closed my eyes, trying to rest, but felt his gaze on me. I flicked my eyes open, and he was still there.

"You need something?"

"No. I mean yes. I mean, I just wanted to say…I just wanted to say thank you."

"Thank you?" Holy crap, my head hurt. I closed my eyes again, praying that maybe I could take a quick nap before we had to go to group therapy. "Thank you for what?"

"For sticking up for me, I guess. No one's—no one's ever done that for me before."

I could hear the cocky sound of Tomas' laughter trail in all the way from the next room. I figured he was talking about me, and from the sound of it, he was making quite a few of the facts up.

"Look." I sucked in my breath as my pillow pushed up against my bruised head. "It wasn't entirely for your benefit, you know. I sorta wanted to beat the crap out of him ever since I saw him."

"Yeah?" He laughed, a high, breathy sound that made him seem younger than his fourteen years. "Well, you wouldn't be the first, I guess. Tomas always has it in for someone around here."

"I noticed."

"No way you'd do that just for me, it's just that — I appreciate it, is all."

"Don't mention it. Okay? It was no sweat." I rolled over.

"...Can I get you something? An icepack for your lip? Here— you want my pillow?" All of a sudden I felt his hands underneath my head as he tried to stuff his pillow underneath my head.

"Ow!" I cried, as his hand pressed into the very spot that hurt the most. "Cut it out!" I batted him away and threw his pillow back on his cot.

"Oh my god, I'm so sorry." He wrung his hands, his face contorted in a look of pure dismay. "I'm an idiot... I'm so sorry."

The way he said it reminded me of the stray puppies that used to beg for scraps around Bravo Hills. When you went to pet them, they'd duck their heads, like they figured you were going to hit them or something.

I sighed and sat up a little. "You're not an idiot. I kind of hurt my head this morning and I just wanted to chill out a bit before rec time was over."

He nodded and dropped his eyes. He began rubbing those scars on his arms, like he did at breakfast. They were thick and ropy—and they spread all the way up to his left ear, which, up close, was burned so badly that it was deformed — like candle wax melting into the side of his head.

What happened to this kid?

"Does Tomas always mess with you?"

"No. I mean, yeah. I mean, like I said, Tomas messes with everyone," he said, shrugging. "I guess I just stick out more than most kids because I'm so crazy."

"You don't seem that crazy," I said slowly. "Besides, you said yesterday that everyone around here is."

"Yeah, I guess I did." He laughed, only his eyes weren't laughing. "…The Hall just does that to kids. Makes 'em road-kill crazy."

I saw a line of preschool kids headed to their cottage earlier that day and it made me sad, seeing their little dirty faces and blank, vacant stares. I felt waterlogged with pain at the thought of Pony in that line, with no one to wipe her face.

God, I had to find her.

I turned to Tim, the sadness hardening to anger. "Tomas is done messing with you, Tim. You just quit worrying about him."

"Why do you say that?"

"Because now, you got me."

Thirteen

break (n): plan to get out.

The days stretched into a week. I felt like half of myself, a shadow, walking around, eating and sleeping, living someone else's life. I felt restless, too, and antsy—waiting for an opportunity, any opportunity.

The routine was easy enough to learn. If you were grade school aged or older, they put you in summer school, whether you liked it or not. The younger kids we hardly saw, because they were at the other end of the compound. After classes we had rec, and some type of sport. In the evening or early afternoon, we had mandatory group therapy—usually run by Seth or another therapist.

Bedtime was the worst. I couldn't sleep.

It was the nightmares, which came every night, one after the other until the alarm woke us for breakfast. Sometimes I'd be screaming, and Tim would shake me awake and I would sit up, drenched in sweat, my heart beating like the baby rabbits I caught for Pony in the fields back home.

The dreams, they were always predictably, sickeningly, the same.

Pony, sleeping on Darla's sunken-in couch, covered in the same dirty clothes I heaped on her the night I escaped the cops. As I watched, somewhere in the room Stan would come creeping up and slowly reach over and begin pulling the clothes off, one by one, until I could see her entire little body curled up into a tiny ball. When I began yelling, his face would turn, and as he grinned in my direction, the features would stretch and twist until finally, when I looked again, I saw that it was really Merlin…

I had to get out of this place.

*   *   *

It was after dinner on a Saturday. I sat on the grass with Tim and a pretty cool black kid named Jaison, during a break from softball, our evening rec activity. It was hot as hell, and all we wanted to do was go back to our cottage and watch TV.

Tim was making daisy chains as he and Jaison swapped gossip, like about who was hooking up with who and which kids had recently come into the Hall. I lay against a wilting tree and half-listened.

The nightmare I had the night before was pretty bad, and the image of Merlin's face, leering and hideous, with stained yellow teeth, was never far from my thoughts. I couldn't escape it. The only thing I could do was pray that Pony was somewhere safe, but I couldn't rely on prayers for much longer. *I had to do something.*

And while I sat there, close to the edge of the compound, an idea began to fester as I studied the walls that surrounded the Hall.

I could escape.

I wanted to kick myself for not thinking about it sooner. It was just too easy. The walls, sure they were tall, maybe ten, twelve feet at the most—but with a little help from someone, a little lift…I could be up and over.

And out.

My feet tingled as I listened to the sounds of cars as they buzzed down the street, people coming and going just as they pleased. Just a few dozen feet away from me lay the one thing I needed most. *Freedom.*

"What do you think, Jesse?" Tim asked, his high-pitched voice crashing through my thoughts. "Do you think I have a chance?"

"Uhh — what?"

"Hey. Earth to Jesse." Jaison threw a dandelion at my head. "Dig this—Timmy E has the hots for Rhonda, you know that girl in Senior Girl's with the lip ring? And he actually thinks he has a chance with her," he said "and I'm trying to tell him—"

"Shut *up*! I do have a chance with her!"

"—And I was telling him that all she does is feel sorry for his crazy white ass—"

"Shut up! She likes me, I'm telling you, Jaison—Guapa told me that she thinks I'm cute."

"Cute, like a little dog is cute. Cute, like your baby cousin is cute. Hey. Whatch *you* think, Jesse?"

It would be so easy.

"Do kids break out of here?" I said in a low voice.

"What?" Tim blinked.

"The wall." I couldn't stop staring at it. "Climbing it. Has it been done before," I repeated patiently.

"Huh?" Jaison snorted. "Oh. Check it out, Timmy E — he's in the breakout phase."

"You can't break out, Jesse," Tim said in a thin, small voice.

"Why not?"

I felt a little bad, because Tim looked like I had socked him or something. Ever since that first day, he had been my shadow. Annoying at first, but after a while I just got used to it. And I hated to admit it, because I never really had very many before, but in a way, Tim had become my friend.

"You just shouldn't mess with it," he said. "Past these walls, it's a really rough neighborhood—*Norteños*, Tomas' territory. Haven't you heard those gunshots at night? Besides, if you got caught, it'd be solitary for days. It's not worth the risk."

"Yeah," Jaison added. "I hate to say it, but Timmy's right. It's practically impossible. There's way too many security guards, and the walls are just too high." He shook his head as if he thought about this many times before. "The only one who can get out of here is the Indian."

"The Indian?" I snapped my head around. "How does he do it? Does he have help?"

Tim placed a daisy chain on top of his head. "No one knows. It really pisses off the staff. One day — he's here. The next day, he's gone."

I got up and walked over to the wall. It was just concrete. The only part that had barbed wire was up toward the front, where all the buildings stood. Out here, once you cleared it, you were out. "He must have had help," I murmured. "Someone to push him up."

I glanced around. The sky was the lightest blue with not a cloud in sight. A few feet away, some kids were playing a volleyball game. Tomas and his gang sat under a large tree over by the cafeteria, laughing and talking, flirting with all the *cholitas* who lived at the Hall. Other girls sprawled on the grass with their pant legs rolled up as far as they could go, trying to catch the last bit of tan before the sun slipped away. Deep in the distance I could see Gary and Lee talking to a Senior Girls' counselor with their backs turned to us.

I could wait, of course. In fact, my practical, analytical side knew I probably should. Wait a couple days until the time was right, maybe even pinch some extra food and supplies for the journey back home. But at the same time, the deepest core of who I was knew that if I waited, I would never again get the courage to do it.

Cowardice. That was the one thing I couldn't handle.

In that instant, I made my decision.

"Guys, I'm gonna do it."

"What?" Tim started rubbing his scars. "Now? You're crazy, Jesse! Just, wait a few days and let's think about it. Jesse—you'll be caught, I'm telling you."

"No, Tim." I scanned the perimeter with slow deliberation one last time, my heart pounding in my ears. "It should be now, when there aren't any security guards around," I whispered. I stood up and began backing closer to the wall.

Slowly.

Slowly.

"Shit," Tim pulled on Jaison's shoulder. "I think he's really going to do it. Talk some sense into him — he's gonna get busted."

"Not if I do it before anyone notices," I said as I inched closer and closer, until my body was enveloped by the wall's steep shade.

Tim craned his neck around, watching for Gary and the other staff. "It's a rule—if anyone's caught within five feet of the wall, it's an instant infraction," he said quickly. "And if they catch you trying to scale, it's solitary."

"I'll take my chances." I kept my eyes on Gary. So far, so good—he still looked deep in conversation with the lady counselor. "Jaison, I'm going to need a lift up. Will you do it?"

"Lord Almighty." He stood up and brushed the grass off his pants with a scared expression on his face. "What you need me to do?"

"Just — just, when I turn around to the wall, hoist my legs up with your hands." Sweat began to trickle down my back. "Do you think you can handle that?"

"Yeah." He walked backward with me. "I got ya."

"You don't even know where you are, Jesse." Tim's eyebrows furrowed together. "How're you going to find your way back home?"

"I'll figure it out." At this point, that was the least of my worries.

I was so close to the concrete blocks that I could reach out and touch them if I wanted.

So. Close.

"Wait!" Tim bounced up and dug his fingers into his hair. The daisy chain fell off onto the ground. "Don't leave me out…what do you want me to do?"

Jaison and I pretended to be deep in conversation as some kids in Tomas' group looked our way. "You can keep your eyes peeled, Tim," I said. "Just have my back, you got it?"

"Okay." I could tell from the sound of his voice that he was bummed.

"Ready, Jaison?" I whispered. He nodded.

"Good. Okay, one, two, three!"

I spanned the rest of the distance and reached my arms up, trying to find a rough spot to hang on to. Jaison bent over and laced his fingers together, and I stepped into his hands, leaning my body against the wall as he hoisted me up.

"Quick! Quick!" Tim hissed. "Before someone looks!"

I stretched my fingers as far as they could go, but I was still a couple feet short. "It's not enough!" I called. "It's too tall."

"I told you," Jaison said below me, trying to push me up as far as he could. "Hold on—Tim, come on over here and help me throw him up."

I felt Tim's hands underneath my other foot and bent my knees, ready to jump when they threw me.

Come on, come on...

"Hey!" The sound of people shouting came from behind me. "Someone's trying to escape!"

"Sampson!" Gary's voice thundered from across the field.

I heard the thump of footsteps on grass and began to panic. "Now, Jaison! Now!"

"Stop! Stop!"

And all of a sudden, I was airborne. For one brief second, I could see the road on the other side, see the people in their cars. I reached out and caught the edge with my fingertips.

"Push me! Hurry!" I yelled as I slipped downward. My feet flailed helplessly below as they struggled to find something to catch hold of.

"Sampson!" Gary's voice boomed closer. "Get down from there right now or there will be major consequences!" I could hear his heavy set of keys jangle with each stride. "Get down! Now!"

I felt for Jaison's palms with my feet and braced as he sent me up one last time. This time I threw my arms over the edge and managed to scrabble up onto the narrow ledge.

Ah.

I tossed my head back, and saw the angry faces of Gary and the lady counselor down below, and the wide, shocked expressions of the other kids as they ran closer to watch. A few whistled and cheered me on.

I nodded to Jaison in thanks. Gary's hands were already clamped down on his shoulders, but he just winked up at me in reply. My eyes met Tim's, and he forced a smile. I grinned back, and without so much as another glance, jumped down to the broken, weedy sidewalk below.

Painpainpainpainpain…

It was quite a fall, and I hit it hard.

My body rolled across the sunbaked sidewalk, and as I stopped myself with my palms, I could taste the dust as it clouded and billowed around me.

My knee throbbed from where it hit during impact. I staggered as I stood up, and swerved around a mom pushing a stroller. An old guy pushing an ice-cream cart stopped and backed against the wall to let me pass. The traffic was thick, but if I was careful enough, I could dodge them, and make my way over to the rundown apartments across the road.

"Stop right there!" Three security guards were running in my direction, with their billy clubs in their hands. "Don't move!"

Oh, crap. I hadn't counted on security guards on the *other* side of the perimeter.

The sun shone in my eyes, I turned on my heel and ran into the traffic, horns blaring as the cars screeched to a stop. I was halfway across when I felt hands grasp the waist of my jeans. I struggled against them but it was too late.

I could see the startled eyes of the drivers as the guards held my arms behind me and pushed me forward. "Come on, kid. It's not safe for you to be out here," the one who caught me said. "Let's go back."

I limped along, trying to keep up with them as they dragged me along. "Ow — let me slow down," I panted.

It was impulsive, what I did, and I knew right then that I should have listened to Tim.

We rounded the corner and the Emerson Hall sign loomed above us, the barbed wire on top of the chain-link fence glittering in the sunlight. I may be going back, but I'd keep trying.

I'd find a way out.

Fourteen

solitary (n): alone.

"This'll teach you to screw with the rules around here," said Gary, as he threw me into the room they used for solitary.

They kept me locked in there the whole night.

The moon was high overhead by the time I gave up thumping on the door, yelling to get let out. When I did finally try to fall asleep, I couldn't, partly because of the adrenaline that still coursed through my body and partly because of the nightmares that hid in wait for me each time I closed my eyes.

Dawn crept through the lone skylight and bathed the room in a pearly gray. Bit by bit, I watched as the fragile pastels of blues and pinks gave way to the summer sunshine. My fingers twitched, and I itched to draw, yearned to see the Sun once more climb up over the Sierra Nevadas of home so I could capture it on paper.

Home. I wanted to be home.

Keys clinked from the other side of the door, and a moment

later the door opened. Instantly, my room filled with the salty, velvety smell of breakfast food.

"Knock, knock. I hear you like bacon, so I brought a whole plate of it." Seth, the shrink from that first day, pushed through, carrying a tray of scrambled eggs, toast, and a mountain of bacon. He set the tray down on the one table by my bed and pushed his glasses up on his nose, assessing me. "You okay?" he said in a soft voice. He touched my knee, which was bandaged from the scrapes.

I flinched. It wasn't broken, but it still hurt. "No, I'm not *okay*." The sight of Seth standing there in his clean plaid shirt, loafers, and sunburnt nose just plain pissed me off. I swiped a fistful of bacon and popped one into my mouth.

"Were you in here the whole night?"

I nodded.

He sat on the very edge of the cot and pressed the tips of his fingertips together. "I'm sorry. That shouldn't have happened."

"You think that shouldn't have *happened*?" I felt my voice raise an octave. "They restrained me, for a fucking hour." My eyes burned at the memory. "Said I was acting suicidal, said I was being a threat to myself and others."

"Doc?" We both looked toward the door as I recognized one of the day security guards positioned outside of my room. "Do you need assistance?" he asked, eyeing me.

Seth exhaled swiftly. "Thanks, Fred — I think I've got it here." He smiled quickly and motioned him back. "You can close the door and wait outside, Jesse will behave himself — right Jesse?"

I glowered at him.

"Go on, Fred," Seth repeated in a calm voice. "We'll be okay."

Fred gave me one more disapproving glare before closing the

door with a loud *click*.

Seth leaned back against the wall and turned to me, an anxious, earnest expression on his face. "This place is not meant to be a prison."

"It sure seems like it."

"You shouldn't have been restrained and put in here. It was unnecessary and inappropriate."

"Why are you here, Seth?" I asked finally. "You gonna lecture me, on why I shouldn't escape and how I need to follow the rules?"

"No. Actually, I'm not." He gave me a hesitant smile. "And I didn't just come in here to bring you breakfast. I came because I have some good news for you."

"Good news?" I tried to fight the hopeful fluttering in my chest. "What?"

"Your social worker's coming here. You get to talk to your sister today."

*   *   *

I couldn't believe it. I had to give Seth credit for following through.

He led me to the main building, where all of the administrative and therapist's offices were located. We walked into an empty room.

"Good luck," Seth said with a wink. "I'll wait outside."

"I'm Cherine." A woman wearing a flowing skirt and sandals stood up. "Nice to meet you."

"Jesse." I hesitated before taking her outstretched hand.

She smiled and held out the phone. "I have someone who

wants to talk to you."

I looked at her with my heart pounding and she nodded. I grabbed it. "Pony?"

"Jesse!"

The connection was a little crackly, but it was her, it was really her.

I turned away from the social worker. "Hey, how are you? I miss you so much. I'm going to come and get you pretty soon. Okay?"

"Jesse, where did you go? I hid like you said, but the lady and the cops found me."

My throat felt tight.

"I know. It was like a game, remember? You did real good. I had to—I had to leave for a while. Take care of some stuff. But I'm coming back. Real soon."

"I want to show you my room. Jesse, my bedspread has ponies on it. And it's pink. Yesterday we went to the zoo—"

"—Have you been sleeping okay?" I sucked in my breath, the guilt over losing the backpack rushing back to me. "I–I tried bringing you your little horse, but she got misplaced. Don't you worry, Pony. I'll get her back."

"That's okay, Mama Karen bought me a new one, all white, with real glass eyes. I named her Snowball."

A new one? She didn't even skip a beat when she told me. And...*Mama Karen*? I decided to let that one go.

"Have you—" I hesitated. I was almost too afraid to find out. "Have you seen anyone from the neighborhood lately? Like... Merlin?"

"Merlin? Nooo," she said. "I haven't seen him. I haven't seen anyone." Her voice dropped. "Not even Mommy."

"Are you sure?"

"Yup."

I felt my chest lighten. Merlin was always so full of shit. So he didn't know where Pony lived, then.

Pony was safe.

I heard fumbling in the background and a woman's voice. "Crystal, sweetie, it's time to get off the phone, okay? Time for dance. Tell him we'll talk to him later."

"Look, Pony. Tell your *foster mother* to get on the phone, please." I bit my lip. "Tell her—"

"Bye-bye, Jesse. I gotta go to my ballet class. I'm wearing a tutu. I love you, call me back, okay?"

More fumbling, and then the line went dead in my ear. I stood there for a second, letting the dial tone just buzz in my ear. Finally, I hung up the phone and glowered at the social worker who sat across from me.

"What the fuck was that? And why are they calling her Crystal?"

She leafed through the file with a stricken face. "Well, Jesse. Crystal is her *name*."

"No, it's not."

As far as I was concerned, Pony was her name. Period.

I blew out the air in my cheeks. "When are you moving me there?"

"Oh, son. I need to explain. This foster family doesn't take older boys. Look, I need to tell you, you're not moving anytime soon."

I felt the blood drain from my face. "Can't you at least move me back to Truckston?"

"We're working on it. Unfortunately, all the foster homes taking older children are full. Besides your aunt, there's no other family."

"I'll be eighteen in a couple years. Doesn't that count for anything? I can take care of her, I've done it before — done it her whole life." I stood up, my fists in a ball. "At least find a home where we can be placed together."

"I'm sorry. I tried." She stood up and reached a hand out to me. "I know you're angry. I would be too."

I shirked my arm away. "Place us together."

"It's not that easy, Jesse. You're…you're old. You have a history of violence—"

"I *what?!*"

She drummed her fingers nervously against her throat. "The incidents you've had here, in Emerson—they've all been documented. I think we need to sit down and look at your options. There are some very good group homes out there for you, which teach young people all about independent living skills—"

"That's bullshit!"

I turned around and threw open the door. Seth was leaning against the wall across from us. He looked at me and lifted his eyebrows.

Cherine poked her head out of the doorway. "Wait! I was going to get your mom on the phone from jail. Don't you want to talk to her?"

"No. I sure as hell *do not.*" I strode down the hallway in wide, angry steps. "Take me back, Seth," I said. I pressed my lips together. It was all I could do to hold it in. "Take me back to the cottage."

Fifteen

meet (v): encounter.

I would have thought that talking to Pony would have made me feel better, but it only made me feel worse. I tried to convince myself that I was glad, no, *thankful* that she was safe, being cared for, and it seemed that for now at least, she was safe from Merlin and Beto.

I *should* have been happy about it.

It's just, I didn't know what to even do anymore—and staying at Emerson couldn't be an option. Maybe I couldn't live with Pony, but I could at least find my way back home. I needed to make things right with Beto.

Breaking out wasn't an option, Tim had said. And he was right—I *did* get caught, but only because I was too hasty. This time I had a different plan.

* * *

The next day at lunch, I worked up the courage to sit down next to the Indian.

"Hi," I said. "Mind if I join you?"

He just glanced at me and took another bite of his enchilada. His hair was braided into a thick, long coil down his back, and his nose hooked into a thin, narrow arch.

"How's it going?" I asked. "Are those enchiladas as bad as Tim says they are?"

He shook his head and looked away. His silence unnerved me.

"Uh." I swallowed. "I hear—I hear that you know how to get out of the place. Escape. That you do it a lot."

He kept his head down, his mouth full of food.

"Can you at least tell me how you do it? I mean, you don't actually scale the walls by yourself, do you? How do you ditch the security officers on the other side? Do they have some type of schedule?"

This time he lifted his head and gave me a dark, penetrating stare. "Do you mind? I'm trying to eat."

His voice was deeper than I expected and I got the shivers. "Oh. Sorry."

This was becoming awkward, but I didn't come this far to give up. I leaned in. "I could pay you."

He lifted an eyebrow.

"If you took me with you. You know, the next time you… leave." I clenched my hands together under the table. "I gotta get out of here."

His face was blank. I couldn't tell whether he was about to deck me or take me up on my offer. "You have money?"

"Well…no. Not right now. But I could work for it. Once I'm

on the outside."

He shook his head. "No. I work alone." A shadow came over his eyes. "Besides, my days of escaping are over. I'll be eighteen in a month, and then…"

He quit talking and took another bite.

"…And then— what?"

"And then I'm out of here for good."

"Well, that's a good thing, right?" I said, forcing a nervous laugh. "Getting out of this place—isn't that what we all want?" I smiled a little. "You're lucky, you'll be free of the system. You got big plans?"

He took his napkin and wiped his mouth with slow deliberation. "Nope."

And with that, he stood up, picked up his tray, and left the cafeteria.

Damn. Guess I was back to square one.

* * *

That night, Senior Boys cottage was watching Empire Strikes Back, which I'd seen like a million times. Tim was driving me nuts, jabbering in my ear the entire time, and the metal chairs were killing my back. Gary was dozing, his chair tilted up against the wall.

Silently, I got up, stretched, and headed toward the back door.

Gary cricked open an eye. "Where do you think *you're* going?"

"The john," I said. "Gotta take a leak."

"Hurry, Sampson." He stifled a big yawn and glanced at his watch. "No funny business — I'm timing you."

I walked toward the bathrooms, turned a quick left and, when he wasn't looking, opened the back door quietly and stepped outside.

I wasn't planning on any funny business, but I wanted to catch a glimpse of the stars and feel the night air for a second. I looked up. Only problem, there were so many lights that you couldn't see any stars—nothing but the orange glow of the city.

This place was getting to me. It was hard to be inside so much, hard to be surrounded by so many kids, with their problems and rage which rose from their bodies like steam off hot asphalt.

I was just about to go back inside, when I noticed a swift movement over by the east side of the compound. I squinted and focused my eyes—it looked like a figure, running.

Well, I'll be damned—someone was breaking out.

Before I knew it, I was running, chasing after the moving shadow, until I neared a solitary bungalow over on the edge of the west side, where they taught preschool to the little kids.

I looked around, breathing heavily. The shadow had disappeared. The only movement was the flicker of lights shining through the windows of the different cottages, where everyone was having their weekend movie night.

I was about to turn back when I heard sniffling. I spun my body around, trying to locate the noise. "Is anyone there?" I whispered.

The sniffling stopped.

A thin trail of smoke wafted from behind the bungalow.

I walked around the corner and saw a girl with long black hair sitting against the building, her body partially hidden by the thick juniper bush that grew against it.

She looked up at me, and took a long drag on her cigarette.

"Go away," she said in a lilting, accented voice. "Find your own spot. This is mine." She wiped her nose.

I stood there, dumbfounded. I had never seen this girl before. Through the shadows, I thought she looked like one of the *cholitas* who hung with Tomas and his crew, but I couldn't be sure.

I crouched down beside her, hoping my body wasn't visible from a distance. "Aren't—aren't you worried about getting caught?" I asked.

She gave a short, smoky laugh. "No, but you should be."

"Why?"

She shot me a dismissive glance and took another puff. "Cause I know how this place runs. And I already know you don't." She flicked her cigarette onto the dead grass.

On impulse, I stretched my foot over and stubbed it out. "Why would you say that?"

She looked like a cat, with tilted, dark eyes and a small mouth. She raised her eyebrows with an amused, superior expression. "*Eres el gabacho loco.*"

Loco. Crazy.

"I'm not crazy." I said it a little louder than I wanted to.

"Oh yeah? ...Says *el gabacho* who hangs out with crazy Timmy E, and starts fights with Tomas. ...Says *el gabacho* who tries to break out in the middle of the frickin' daytime." Her small, pointed white teeth gleamed in the darkness. "It doesn't get any crazier than that."

I stiffened, feeling my blood begin to rise. "I think you'd be crazy not to try to break out of here."

She laughed. "Why? What's the difference? Same old shit, inside or outside."

"You don't care if you're here?"

"No." Her eyes were dull as she looked across toward the wall. "This place is as good as any."

I knew that I should get back, that at any minute, Lee would realize I was gone and would sound the alarm. He'd get busted for letting me go, and I'd find myself in solitary again. But for some reason, my legs wouldn't budge.

I peered closer and saw that her eyes were swollen and red. "Then why are you crying?"

"None of your damn business, crazy white boy." She wiped her eyes, smudging her heavy black makeup.

"Saaaamp-son!" I saw the sweep of a flashlight stretch out over the west side of the complex.

"Shit. I'm gonna be busted."

"Told you." I could hear the smirk in her voice.

"...Sampson!"

"Shit!" I flattened my body against the side of the wall, praying that he wouldn't spot me. Any second and there would be every security guard in the place hunting me down. "What—what should I do?"

She paused for a moment. "Come here," she said with a disgusted sigh. She pulled me down next to her and the prickly leaves of the juniper scratched my arms and face as I tried to hide my long legs behind it. ""They'll do a sweep of your cottage, first. Then they'll radio the other cottages to make sure you didn't slip inside one of those. You've got a couple minutes before the security guards make their way over here."

Up close, she smelled of cigarettes and cinnamon. Through the shadows, I could see the sparkle of her gold eye shadow and the path where her tears slid down her cheek.

"Then what?" I breathed.

She nodded toward the administrative buildings. "You remember LaVonda, that black chick who did your intake?"

"Yeah."

She stretched her neck across me and watched as Lee and two security guards walked the east perimeter.

"She's the noc nurse. She gives the mental kids their meds at night. Run, right now, into her office and tell her that dinner tonight gave you massive *chorillo* and you need some meds. Tell her you didn't know where else to go. That way you won't get in trouble for being gone. Trust me — works every time."

"*Chorillo*," I repeated carefully. The word wasn't familiar to me. "Okay." I stood up, and brushed the sticky twigs off of me. "Thanks. What about you—will you be caught?"

"My cottage counselor and I have an understanding." She waved her hand away. "I'll be fine. Now, *go*."

I braced to run, and then turned back around. "I'm Jesse. What's your name?"

"Oh, no." Another throaty laugh. "I don't do names — especially with white boys."

I could still hear them calling me. It might be too late.

The whole night felt surreal, and a boldness coursed through my veins, making me feel suddenly, completely alive. "Tell me your name — I'm not leaving until you do."

She huffed, and looked nervously toward the flashlights. "Fine. It's Aurora. But you never saw me here, *entiendes*?"

I nodded. "Got it." I began to sprint toward the offices when I turned back around one more time. "Wait — *chorillo*; what does that mean?"

"Diarrhea", she said with a grin.

Sixteen

tattoo (n): permanent, lasting mark on your
body.

Girls. We got to see them during class and at mealtimes, that's it. Guess they didn't want to run the risk of girls getting pregnant while in custody. Even so, there were lots of hookups, according to Tim Emmett, but if you got caught by staff, you faced major consequences.

For the last twenty-four hours, my mind had been consumed with the image of the girl I met behind the preschool bungalow late last night. It was such a shock to have run into her, and even though she made it clear she wanted nothing to do with me, I found myself thinking about her, wondering why she had been crying. I always hated it when girls cried, because I always wanted to fix it, and usually I never could.

I looked for her in the halls the next day, hoping I'd catch a glimpse of her in the daylight. She wasn't in any of my summer school classes, and I didn't know any of the girls well enough to ask about her.

*   *   *

Jaison had started a little side business giving the guys tattoos when staff wasn't looking. He claimed he learned how to do it from a cousin who'd been in prison.

I was one of his first customers.

We waited until everyone was asleep, including Gary who was snoring in the rec room, before we snuck into the showers. Tim, Jaison, and I sat on the cold tile floor in the darkness. Tim shined a flashlight as Jaison worked on my upper arm.

"So, Jess. W—hatcha getting inked?" Tim's voice echoed off the bathroom tiles.

"Hush, Tim — keep it down." Jaison squinted as he peered closer to my arm. "Shine the flashlight closer."

"Like that?" The flashlight shined in my face before settling on the spot on my arm.

"Yeah," he said, grunting as he worked. "Exactly like that."

My arm beaded up with blood with every jab of the needle. "I met a girl the other day."

"Yeah?" Jaison glanced up at me, his lips spreading into a grin. "Good for you. She like you?"

I felt the corners of my mouth curve as I remembered her expression just before I ran off. "I don't know…" I shrugged. "I think there might have been something there."

"Jesse's in looovveee," sang Tim.

"I think she's new—I've never seen her before. She—I think she's a *cholita*," I said, grimacing against the pain. "At least she looked that way."

Tim laughed. "Maybe you guys can double date with me and Rhonda when we all get out of here."

"You are dreaming about Rhonda." Jaison rolled his eyes at me. "I swear, it's like talking to a two-year-old sometimes."

I sucked in air through clenched teeth. "Almost done?"

"Okay. All done. How'd I do?"

I turned to look. *Pony*, said the tattoo in scrawling, slanting letters.

My arm was throbbing. But somehow, the pain made me feel better, made me remember her. "Wow, Jaison. It's perfect."

"Keep it clean. It'll hurt like a mother for the first few days."

"Thanks, man."

He wiped my upper arm with a wet paper towel. "Just be sure to keep it hidden, Jess. I don't want to get busted for this." He patted the homemade tattoo needle. "So, does this girl of yours have a name?"

I looked down. She said she didn't do names, whatever that meant. I had to pry it out of her. "It's Aurora," I admitted finally. "You know her?"

Jaison and Tim stared at me with frozen expressions for about five seconds until they both collapsed against each other into silent, racking laughter.

I felt my cheeks flame crimson. "What?"

"That is the most hilarious thing I have ever heard," said Tim between breaths.

"*Why* is that hilarious?" I said, coloring. "Do you know her or something?"

Jaison's face scrunched in glee. "Timmy, dude here's asking if we know her! Do we know her, Tim?"

"What's the matter?" I demanded. "Tell me, guys."

Tim's face sobered. "We know her, all right—and you couldn't have picked a better *mamacita* to crush on, Jesse James."

I couldn't take it anymore. "*Why*?"

Jaison bent closer to me. "Aurora—with long, black hair, and those kind of sexy, slanty eyes?"

"I think so." I blushed again. "I mean, it was dark."

"Kind of short, but with big…" his fists made a squeezing motion up by his chest.

"Cha-chas," Tim added helpfully.

"I don't—I don't know, exactly!" I was growing impatient.

"Jesse." Jaison rested a hand on my shoulder. "Aurora is Tomas' cousin."

I felt the blood drain from my face.

That explained why she acted so frosty around me, and how she knew who I was. Tomas and I had managed to stay away from each other. We were warned not to fight again and the staff kept a close eye on us. But like a taut rope, the tension was there. Always. The fat lip I had given him was almost gone and I would welcome the chance to give him another one.

"Crap."

Tim patted my shoulder sympathetically. "Steer clear of that one."

"Dangerous," Jaison said. He shook his head. "Don't do it."

I didn't want to talk anymore. "Come on, guys." I stuck my head out of the bathroom door. The TV was still on, and I could see Lee's sleeping body sprawled out on the couch. "We better get back to bed before someone wakes up."

"No wait, Jaison," said Tim. "I want to go next. I wanna ink my dad's name. He's locked up."

Jaison crawled after me. "No, Timmy E. Tomorrow night. Okay?"

"Okay," he mumbled.

*   *   *

Despite what the guys said, I found myself looking for Aurora over the next couple of days. It was like she disappeared into thin air.

And then, on the third day, I saw her.

We were walking out of group therapy and heading toward the cottages for evening rec. I stopped to get some water at the drinking fountain when I had the prickling sensation of eyes upon me. I looked up, and there she was, standing with a cluster of girls over on the blacktop.

Our eyes locked, and I felt my heart hurl itself against my ribcage. She gave me a swift, deliberate look and then folded back in with her friends. She was even more gorgeous in the daytime.

Tim came up behind me and stopped dead in his tracks when he saw where I was looking. "Oh, no," he groaned.

I finished drinking, wiped my mouth and began walking in the opposite direction. "There's no crime in looking," I said, irritated.

"Just as long as it's *looking*," Tim countered.

I stopped walking and, acting on intuition, whipped my head around.

There. I caught her looking again. This time I gave her a smile.

She scoffed, that same disgusted expression as the other night and then turned her back on me.

That was it. I never could turn down a challenge.

"There's no harm in talking," I told Tim, and turned around on my heels and strode back over to where she was standing.

"Aw, man." Tim covered his face. "You have a frickin' death wish, country boy."

There were about ten of them, laughing and talking in a tight cluster. Veronica, a girl with skunk-dyed hair and bad acne, noticed me standing there and narrowed her eyes. "What you looking at, *gabacho*?"

The entire group of girls fell silent, watching me. Aurora kept her head down. I looked from her to Veronica. "Uh…I wanted to talk to *her*."

The girls widened their eyes, and then laughed. "Here you go," said Veronica, pushing her forward. "I didn't know you two were *acquainted*." More laughter.

"Hi." I swallowed. "It's Aurora, right?"

She scowled at me and crossed her arms. I took her by the elbow and walked us a couple of feet over.

"What are you *doing*?" she hissed.

I had no idea what I was doing.

"I—I just wanted to say thanks for saving my butt the other night."

"You already said thank you." She pulled her dark hair off of her face and glanced around.

"I guess I thought that we could talk sometime. You know, be friends."

"We can't be friends," she said in a low voice.

Her friends twittered behind us and I saw Tim waiting for me out of my peripheral vision. "When I found you — why were you crying?" I asked softly.

She lifted her brown eyes to mine and I saw her pupils dilate. Her lips were full and shiny with pink lip-gloss. Looking at her, I felt I could hardly breathe.

"Look, just leave me alone."

I felt a shadow fall over us. "Is there a problem here, *prima*?"

Tomas and four of his homeboys stood behind us. His face held a murderous expression. I was about to face him, pop off with some smart-ass comment, when Aurora shot me a quick, pleading look.

"No. No problem here," she said, that cool, icy expression back in place. "*Este gabacho* was just leaving. Weren't you?" she said pointedly.

He looked from Aurora to me. "Good. Then *leave*, Trailer Park. Go back over with your own kind."

I stood stock still, my fists tingling in anticipation. "I was just leaving," I said through gritted teeth. I turned to look at her one more time. "Bye, Aurora," I said. "Talk to you later."

I turned on my heels and walked away.

Seventeen

```
kiss (v): to caress one another with the lips.
```

Since it was summer, they offered these extra classes for us to take in the evenings. Most of them were pretty pathetic: *Personal Grooming, Safe Sex Seminar, Independent Living Skills, Summer Book Club*. But one is particular caught my eye—Intro to Drawing. The roster promised that everyone in the class would get their own set of charcoals, paints, and a fresh pad of paper. I would get to draw again, really *draw*.

I was the first to sign up.

On the day it started, though, group therapy had run late and I was one of the last to enter the classroom.

My heart skipped a beat.

The only seat open was one in the very back, next to Aurora.

"Hi," I said, and sat down at the empty desk. "Is this seat taken?"

Her face paled when she saw me.

"No," she said, all at once composing herself. She arched her perfectly penciled eyebrows. "Go ahead. It's a free country, last time I checked."

"I'm not so sure about that. There are some pretty thick walls around this dump." I tried my best to act cool, casual, but being so close to her didn't make it easy.

The teacher, a guy named Mr. Vance with bleached, feathered hair, stood at the front. "Class? Time to begin," he called.

The classroom was a noisy buzz of kids talking and laughing. "So, do you like to draw?"

"A little." She kept her body erect with her head straight ahead, as if she didn't want anyone to see her talking to me. "You?"

"A little."

I could feel the electricity crackle between us.

"Everyone? Quiet now, please." Mr. Vance was supposedly some famous guy from Beverly Hills who owned his own art studio. He had so much plastic surgery that when he spoke, his face didn't move. "Now, let me take a quick roll call to see who's here."

I shifted my eyes in Aurora's direction. Her black hair hung like a curtain over her profile, but I could still see the curl of her eyelashes, the curve of her lips. God, was she fine.

She caught me looking and ducked her head, softly shaking it side to side.

"Every day this week, I catch you staring at me, *gabacho*." She wet her lips with her tiny pink tongue. "Stare and stare and stare. All the time, I'm thinking, what's the matter, do I look funny to him or something?"

I had to smile. The girl was good, a pure genius at playing the game.

"You've been staring, too," I pointed out. "I've noticed. What's the matter, do *I* look funny to *you*?"

She tilted her head and continued drawing. "Maybe you do. *Maybe*... I'm just trying to figure you out. But Tomas, Tomas says to stay away—says you're gay."

"I'm not gay."

It was just like Tomas to say something like that.

"It's cool if you are, though. The Indian is. Lots of people are."

"I'm not gay, okay?" I felt my teeth grit.

When I looked over at her, I saw that she was laughing silently.

"So you're messing with me, huh? Is that it? You think you're funny?" I reached over and scribbled a line across her paper.

She made a face at me. "*Callate*," she chided. "I'm trying to *listen*."

"...I would like to assess everyone's skill level," Mr. Vance was saying, "So I will be giving everyone fifteen minutes to sketch any-thing you like. You may begin."

I grabbed the sketch pad and began drawing in swift, deliber-ate strokes. It felt so good to draw again, and the pencil felt like home in my hand. The feel of the lead gliding over the paper, the sound of the pencil point scratching as I shaded in the edges, the shiny gray smudges on my fingers and the heel of my hand—it was comforting, being there, lost inside my own head, my own pictures.

As I got caught up in the drawing, I sensed her watching me. I glanced up and we made eye contact. Her eyes widened, and I knew we both felt it. Heat. Pure, white heat.

"Hey," I whispered. "Show me your picture."

"Nuh-uh. That's not how I operate. Show me yours, first." She lifted her eyebrows suggestively.

After a moment's hesitation, I held it out for her.

"Dang," she said under her breath. "That's good. Real good."

It still needed more work, I thought, and added a bit more shading to the mountains. The landscape was something I've been drawing ever since I could hold a pencil. The view from my home at sunset, with the sun shining all golden on the river's currents, and the mountains staining purple with each passing minute.

Home, except without the druggie trailer park.

"Your turn." I nudged her.

She held out her drawing. It was a wolf, sitting on a rock overlooking a lake. The lifelike detail was incredible.

"Wow. How did you do that?" I asked.

She shrugged, pleased with my compliment. "I draw all the time. And I love to draw animals. Especially wild ones. They're free, you know? Free and innocent." She looked down kind of shyly. "You remind me of a wolf. Something in your eyes." She traced her picture slowly. "They're blue, but green in the center."

My throat felt dry. "Meet me later." Crazy boldness coursed through me, and before I could think, the words were out. "Tonight."

One of Aurora's friends, a girl they called Squeaky, turned around from a few rows in the front to give me the once-over. She frowned at us.

Aurora ducked her head and hunched over her paper. "No. You're crazy," she whispered. "It's not even possible."

"Sure it is." My lips hovered over her ear. "Eleven o'clock. By the bungalow. I'll be waiting."

*   *   *

I slipped out right before eleven. A summer thundershower had passed through a few days ago, and the air was still thick and humid. I ran from building to building, but at least this time I had done my research, and knew that the security started their patrols on the other side of the compound. I'd have about a half an hour, at the most. I prayed she'd be there.

When I rounded the corner, I felt a jolt when I saw her sitting in the shadows against the side of the bungalow. "You came," I said.

"You sound surprised."

"Actually, I am."

I sat down next to her, all at once nervous and uncertain. She shivered and hugged her knees with her arms.

"You cold?" I reached out to touch her arm and she flinched. "Hey. I'm not going to hurt you."

"We shouldn't be doing this," she said in a low voice.

I dropped my hand and forced a soft laugh. "And what are we doing? We're just talking."

She shrugged and looked away, out toward the surrounding neighborhood. A dog barked in the distance as we fell silent.

She wet her lips before she spoke. "…You ever want a different life?"

Her question took me by surprise. "Yeah. I mean, like, always."

She ducked her head. "When I was a little girl, you know what I wanted to be?"

"What?"

"A forest ranger." She laughed. "Stupid, huh?"

"Not so stupid."

She smiled and shrugged. "I saw this special on the TV one time, about this forest ranger whose job all day was to live up in a tower, and search for forest fires with binoculars. There were these big green fir trees growing for miles and miles, until you couldn't see no more." When she spoke, I saw a softness in her eyes I hadn't seen before. "Just seemed real peaceful, you know? All that green. All those trees."

I imagined her, the tough *cholita*, standing up in one of those towers, with the wind blowing in her hair, like Rapunzel in the fairy tale. It made me smile.

"You could do that, Aurora."

"No way."

"Why not? You could."

All of a sudden I saw that veil go back up in place behind her eyes, like a wall clicking back into place. I couldn't let that happen, not now, not when we might never get the chance again. In a swift motion, I placed an arm around her shoulder. Holding my breath, I braced myself for her to protest, but instead she rested her head on my shoulder.

I was really doing it—I was holding Aurora.

I kissed the top of her head. "I've never seen a forest before." Her body relaxed against mine. "Just the trees that grow along the river by my house, but they're mostly oaks and sycamores." I thought about the pictures of forests I'd seen, endless acres full of pines and lakes. I imagined us there together, away from all the dirty asphalt, all the buildings and cars. "I'd like to go sometime."

I could feel her heart beat hard against mine. "Yeah?" she whispered back.

I was still reeling from holding her, touching her skin and smelling her hair. She had no makeup on tonight, and it made her look younger, more innocent. She was so beautiful, and in that instant she reminded me of the girl with the sandwiches that day at the park—except Aurora had a fullness, a ripeness about her, like the figs that would drop from the gnarled old tree behind our trailer. In the summer, I would eat them until I was sick.

I gazed at her, with her small upturned nose and lip-glossed mouth. For the first time I noticed a tiny bluish-gray teardrop tattooed by the corner of her left eye. I reached out to trace it with my thumb. "What's this?"

"Oh." She closed her eyes when I touched her. "I got it when my brother was killed."

"What happened?"

"He was shot in front of our house by a rival gang when I was little. When he died, I didn't speak for weeks." She shook her head, her eyes shiny. "But now I just live by my motto, you know? Smile now, cry later."

"I'm sorry."

"Don't be." All at once she forced a smile. "What about you, *gabacho*? You got some new ink, I see."

She took her forefinger and traced it up my arm, until it traveled over my biceps, circling the tattoo, still scabbed over. Her touch was like fire on my skin. "Is she why you're sad?"

I flinched my muscle. "Who?"

"Pony. Your girlfriend. You must miss her, being in here."

I shook my head, the ache sinking to my stomach where it curled up and tensed, hardened and ugly. "Not my girlfriend. My little sister."

"Oh. Is she dead?"

"No. Foster care."

I lay down on the grass, with my face toward the sky. She lay down next to me, the long tendrils of her hair tickling my arms.

"What kind of name is Pony, anyway?"

"Just a name I gave her."

"Why?"

I kept my eyes on the clouds that still lingered.

"When she was just learning to talk, I got her this stuffed pony. I won it at the fair—some stupid game that probably cost more than it was worth, three times over. Anyway. It was pink with a purple mane, and man, did she love that thing. Carried it around with her everywhere, couldn't go to sleep without it. For a while, *pony* was the only word she would say." I smiled as I remembered. "I guess you could say the name stuck."

I reached over and pulled a strand of hair out of her eyes. "Her real name is Crystal. I hate it. She wasn't the first girl in the world to be named after crystal meth, but still, I didn't want her named after my mom's juice."

I moved closer to her, slowly, so as not to scare her.

She blinked, her lashes like cobwebs dusting her face. Lightly, so lightly, she touched my cheek. "You're different, *gabacho*."

Our lips were inches away from each other, and I could feel her breath on my face. "Jesse," I whispered, stroking her jaw with my fingers. "Please. Call me Jesse."

"Jesse." Her body quivered as she stared up at me.

I pulled her head to mine and kissed her. Her mouth tasted like cinnamon, sweet and spicy at the same time.

"I never kissed a white boy, before," she whispered.

"Do I taste different?" I brushed my lips against her throat.

"Better." We wrapped our bodies around each other, and I threaded my fingers through her hair.

She pulled away and stared into my face. "You know what I said about smiling now and crying later?"

"Yeah?"

"This works too."

Eighteen

secret (n): kept from knowledge or view.

I t's fun to keep secrets." Her hot breath blew in my ear.

"It's stupid."

We held hands under the table in art class. For days now, we kept our secret, but it was getting harder every day. There was something addictive about Aurora. When I saw her, I wanted to see her more. When I kissed her, I needed more.

Aurora, Aurora, Aurora.

I was drunk on Aurora, and it was never enough.

Mr. Vance had a still life of fruit we were going to draw and he droned on about perspective. We didn't pay attention.

"Jesse." She smiled at me sideways and drew circles into my palm with her forefinger. "I want to kiss you so bad right now," she whispered.

I shook my head. "I'm sick of sneaking around all the time. You're just afraid of your cousin. Afraid that he'll be mad at you for seeing me, the white boy."

She frowned. "You'd be smart to be afraid of him, too. Tomas—he's bad."

"I know."

"No, I mean, he's really…bad. He could hurt you."

"I'm not scared of that guy." I shot a glance over at her. "I kicked his ass before."

Her eyelashes fluttered. "But I am, Jesse. Be careful around him. Promise me."

"Fine. I promise."

She gave my hand a squeeze.

I gazed at her. It was definitely hard trying to sneak around, steal moments together. But each kiss, each touch, each word we shared together made everything worth it. Every day I woke up, knowing I'd get to see her, was another day that I survived the Hall.

"I have something for you," I whispered.

She gave me a slow smile. "What is it?"

"Here," I said, pulling a piece of paper out of my back pocket. "I drew you something." I felt myself blush as I spoke, so I quickly handed it to her. She gave me a questioning look and unfolded it. "I—I've been working on it for a while."

"Oh, Jesse." She smoothed the paper out on the desk, her breath catching. "It's—it's me." She bit her lip as she looked at it. "It's beautiful. You drew me beautiful."

I breathed lightly, my arms aching to hold her. "You are beautiful, Aurora."

She blinked rapidly. There it was again, that little wall she would occasionally put up in front of me. "I — I love it, Jesse. I do." She snapped her eyes up to mine, her pupils large. "Will you have it?

Will you keep it for me? To — remember me."

I searched her face. "Why would I need to remember you?" I asked in a low voice.

She handed the portrait back to me. "Please. Just in case — if something happened."

I was about to answer her when the door flew open. Jaison and a kid named Elliot rushed in.

"Help! Come quick—Tim Emmett's holed up in the bathroom, freaking out. We think he's on something bad." Jaison was breathless.

I jumped up and ran for the door. Chairs squeaked and feet shuffled as Mr. Vance struggled to keep order.

"Everyone, remain seated," he said as most of the kids filed out. "Class!" He wrung his hands helplessly.

I jogged with Jaison and Elliot down the hall toward the Senior Boys' Cottage. "What happened?" I asked, panting as I ran.

"I'm not sure. His social worker came today and they talked for a long time. When she left he disappeared. Elliot found him hysterical, barricaded in the bathroom. Jess, he's talking crazy, man."

We ran into our dorm. Most of the guys were standing outside of the bathroom while Seth pounded on the door.

"Tim! Stay with me, buddy. Help is on its way." I could hear the sound of Tim sobbing through the locked door.

I grabbed Seth's shoulder. "What's going on?"

He shook his head. "He found out that his dad died, today. In prison. Cancer."

"His dad?"

"Come on Timmy, open up," Jaison yelled. "Yeah," he added, eyeing me. "You know, the one who gave him all those scars?

Frickin' monster, man."

I had noticed during showers that he had thick, ropy scars up and down his back. More on his arms—they looked like burns. He tried to cover them with his towel, but they were impossible to hide completely.

"Tim!" I shouted. "Open the door!"

"Paramedics should be here any minute," Seth breathed. "Tim!" He throttled the doorknob.

"Hold on." The Indian stepped forward, holding a long, thin piece of metal, like a crowbar. "I can get in."

"Shit!" Jaison's eyes bugged out. "Where'd you get that?"

The Indian pushed him aside and jimmied the metal in the doorjamb by the knob. He rammed the door with his shoulder, and we all heard the loud noise of wood breaking. Another ram, and it creaked open.

Tim Emmett was curled up on the bathroom tile, cans of hairspray tossed around him. His face was red and blotchy from crying.

"Tim!" Seth and I rushed forward. I cradled his head in my hands. "What's the matter, buddy? What have you done?" My heart was racing, but I talked to him gently, like I did with Pony when she woke up from a bad dream.

He rolled over, covering his face. "My dad died. My frickin' dad died, Jesse." Shiny tracks of mucus stretched down his cheeks and lips. His pupils were large and dilated. He took a sobbing gasp. "Oh, God, he's dead."

"Hey, hey—it's okay." I rubbed his back.

"Tim, did you sniff these cans?" Seth held his wrist and checked his pulse. "Where'd you get the cans, son?"

"I loved that bastard, but he didn't love me. I loved him, he was my frickin' dad. Oh, God." His body shook with racking, silent sobs.

Seth scooped him up and held him in his arms. "Tim, the paramedics are coming to check you out, and then we'll talk about this, okay? We'll talk about how you feel —"

"— My whole life, all I wanted was for that asshole to love me." He reached over, grabbed a can and flung it against the wall. "I need more, more, goddammit. Please, I'm begging you, please give me something to sniff."

All I could do was rub his leg. Most of the guys from the cottage were crowded at the door, staring with frightened eyes.

Seth smoothed his hair. "No, no, Tim," he said in a soothing voice. "This shit is dangerous. It could kill you. There are better ways to let out the pain. We can talk. I can help you."

Two paramedics in blue uniforms pushed through with a big black bag. "Did he inhale all those cans?" asked the one with the buzz cut.

"I think so," Seth said.

"Tim," said the paramedic. "Can you hear me? Stay with me, Tim."

Right then, his eyes rolled into the back of his head. His lips went slack. "Tim!" They laid him on the tile and knelt over him.

"Come on, Jesse." Seth pulled me up. "Let's give these guys room to work."

I felt queasy. Tears flooded my eyes. "Is he going to be okay? What's wrong with him? Is he going to die?"

Seth steered me out of the bathroom into the cottage. "He's with professionals, Jesse. He's in the best hands."

The paramedics wheeled Tim on a stretcher across the grounds and out the main doors to the ambulance. His face was covered with an oxygen mask. Most of the older kids of the Hall had spilled out of the classrooms and were outside. They all just stood there, frozen.

"Jesse." Aurora ran up and wrapped her arms around my shoulders. "Oh, my God, what happened? Will he be okay?"

I hugged her to me and kissed her hair. A deep sob escaped from my chest, and I hugged her tighter, smoothing the hair down her back.

"I don't know," I murmured.

"Oh, Jesse." She pulled my face to her lips and kissed my cheekbone, my lips. I kissed her back and closed my eyes.

When I opened them, I saw Tomas standing in the middle of the corridor, watching us.

Nineteen

eruption (n): a huge explosion.

For three nights, I fell asleep staring at the empty bed beside me. Sometimes I couldn't sleep at all, with those images of Tim screaming flashing through my head, again and again. Maybe it was worry, maybe it was just because I was dead tired, but I felt strange, like my skin was too tight, and one day I was going to just crawl right out of it.

On the fourth day, Tim just walked into the cafeteria during dinner as if nothing had ever happened. Of course, he left his hospital bracelet on, but still he was back to the old Tim, laughing, talking fast, and joking about what happened.

"I had the hottest nurses," he said as we ate a dinner of cold hamburgers and tater tots in the cafeteria. "This one — Sheri — a real sweet redhead, she made sure to give me extra chocolate puddings."

"Man," said Elliot, "did you get her number?"

"Nah." Tim pushed the food around with his fork. Without a word, he slid the plate to me. I grabbed it, having finished off my burger already, and took a bite. "But the drugs, dude. The drugs they gave me were the best. No more sniffing paint for me, no way. Next time I need a good high, I'll just get myself back to the hospital."

Everyone laughed.

Still, we were all extra gentle with Tim Emmett. Nobody messed with him, and everyone made sure not to mention what happened. Tim was questioned for hours by staff on where he got the cans, but he wouldn't say a word. Extra security guards roamed the halls.

We had group for Senior Boys the following Thursday. I didn't think Tim would show, but he did.

"Hey," I said when he sat down. "I thought Seth said you didn't have to come today."

"No way." He grinned his goofy smile. "I feel great—everything's cool. Besides, how could I miss out on Lisa? Man," he said, patting his heart, "that chick is *so* fine."

Lisa was another psychology intern who ran the group with Seth. She only came every once in a while, and when she did, all the guys went crazy. Too old for me—I didn't go for the cougar thing — and nowhere near as beautiful as Aurora.

"Everyone take a seat," Seth said, as the last few stragglers walked in. "Let's get started."

Seth cracked me up in group. I mean, I respected the guy. He did me right that first day by getting my social worker to come out, and he was really there for Tim Emmett, but the dude was hilarious in group. When a guy would speak, Seth would hunch all over, all serious like, and push his gold-rimmed glasses up on his nose, and nod his head a lot, saying things like, "I see," when people spewed their crap.

He didn't have to worry about me running off my mouth. I wasn't real big on group. Let me rephrase that. I *hated* group. Sure, they could make me go, but they couldn't make me speak. I'd sit there, with my arms crossed, and zone out. To tell you the truth, I wasn't sure how talking about your problems made you feel better. Thinking, talking about my life only seemed to make me feel worse.

"Guys," Seth said when we got started. "I'm sure you all noticed that Tim Emmett decided to join us today." The group erupted into some claps and whistles. "Tim and I have talked extensively about what happened last week, and he felt it was important for him to be here today." Seth smiled and put his hand on Tim's shoulder. "And Tim, I'd just like to say, that I was real worried for your safety. I'm glad you're here. Glad you're with us."

Tim Emmett grinned at all of us. He was eating up the attention.

"Yeah, I mean — hey guys, I'm sorry. I — I fucked up. Whoops," he said holding out his hand, "sorry for using a profanity, Miss Lisa."

Lisa smiled. I guess she was kind of hot, for a shrink. "That's okay, Tim."

"I'm doing real good in therapy, and I know now that the best thing for me is to stick in therapy, work through my issues, and stay off the drugs. Man," he said, shaking his head. "The doc said I could have killed myself."

"Thank you, Tim," Seth said. "I appreciate your sharing."

"Dude, is it true? Were you trying to kill yourself?" Jeremiah, a skinny new kid with bucked teeth, asked.

"Yeah. No. Oh, I don't know." Tim raked his fingers through his hair. "I mean, I've been dealing with shit with my dad since I was, you know, little."

He hugged his knees and rocked forward. Suddenly the air felt denser, as his voice dropped to a hoarse whisper. "The scars on my back, my arms. You know, they still hurt sometimes." His body shuddered. "I'll never understand, like, I can't wrap my brain around it — how a guy can molest his own kid and then light him on fucking fire. How can a dad do that? Huh?'"

The room went dead silent.

Seth cleared his throat, then rearranged his glasses. He put an arm around Tim. "We don't have to discuss this right now if it is making you too emotional, Tim," he said quietly. "Maybe we should do this later."

Tim shook his head. "See, I can't. It's just, it's like an eruption inside of me, all these feelings that keep flowing and flowing and flowing... I can't make them stop. I can't turn them off." He bowed his head and started sobbing. "Fuck! Doing that shit to your own kid."

I felt dizzy and ducked my head forward. Something was wrong with me—I couldn't control my breathing anymore. Big spots of red and black bloomed in my vision, and then I couldn't see my hands in front of me. My breathing came short and quick. The sound of Tim's voice echoed in my ears until I couldn't take it anymore.

"I gotta get outta here," I said, knocking over my chair.

I bolted out of the room.

I ran down the hall, not knowing where to go. All I knew is that I needed to get away, away from Tim, away from the stifling air in that room.

Footsteps closed in fast behind me, and I knew that once they caught me I'd be busted. They'd take away all my hard earned privileges for leaving like that.

"Jesse!" Seth closed the gap between us and grabbed my arm. "You okay?"

I shifted my eyes. "Oh, yeah, I'm fine. I just — it's hot in there."

"You sure?" He tilted his head and studied my face. "Jesse. Would you like to talk about it sometime?" he said in a soft voice.

It was as if he could see right through me.

"What? No. Talk about what?" I could hear the guys messing around in the classroom. "Don't you need to like, get back? They'll tear up the place." I felt my breathing quicken again.

"It's fine. Lisa's got them." He maintained his gaze. "You don't seem fine, son."

"I'm fine, dammit." I felt my anger rise, and it was a good feeling, because it made me feel more in control. "Look, let's just go back in there, Tim needs you right now."

His face was kind. "Tim's going through a hard time, yes. But group is for everyone."

I started walking back to the classroom, my hands deep in my pockets. "You know what, Seth? You worry too much." With each step I took, that big, pulsing shadow stuffed itself back in, back inside. Where it belonged.

Twenty

trouble (n): problematic situation.

We were painting with watercolors that day. I was curious because I'd never done it before. I mainly just stuck with my pencils and charcoals.

The seat remained empty beside me, and I craned my neck toward the door. Mr. Vance took roll call.

"Aurora?" He looked over. "Aurora Ramirez? Does anyone know where she is?"

Guapa, a girl with black lipstick and a pierced tongue raised her hand. "She's sick today, Mr. Vance. Throwing up and shit. She went to the nurse's this morning."

He made a note on his paper.

I was worried.

How long had she been sick? We hadn't seen each other in a couple of days, not since Tomas saw us together. I thought about asking Guapa, but she was in tight with Tomas' crew, and I couldn't risk it.

Toward the end of lunch, I saw Aurora slip into the cafeteria and grab a tray. She looked pale. I got in line to get another glass of milk and stood beside her.

"Hi," I said softly. I looked around to make sure nobody was paying attention. Most of the kids had cleared out with just a few stragglers remaining. "Missed you in class today." I grazed her arm with the back of my knuckles. "Are you okay? Guapa said you were sick."

"Yeah." She edged away from me, and grabbed a serving of green Jell-O. Her eyes were distant. "I'm okay."

She wasn't acting right, and the realization sent waves of tension through my body. I took a step closer. "What's wrong? Did I do something?"

She shook her head violently.

"You can't lie to me, Aurora. I can tell when something's wrong. Is it Tomas?"

"No."

"Well then, what is it?" I reached over and brushed a strand of hair off of her face. "You can tell me anything."

She looked right at me this time. God, her face — she seemed so helpless, like a lost little kid. I wanted to kiss her right there.

She pushed my hand away, and then looked like she regretted it. "Oh, Jesse. It's just — look, this is hard for me. Real hard, because you're a good guy." Her voice cracked. "You know that? You're good. I'm all wrong for you. You can do better than me."

My heart thumped out of my chest. "I'm not that good," I said, trying to smile.

The corners of her mouth drooped. "Jesse."

"What?" My mind spun in circles. I wet my lips. "Are you breaking up with me?" I asked finally.

"Please. Please don't make me explain."

The door to the outside opened and in walked Tomas. He headed straight for us, as if he knew we were there.

"Well, well," he said. "So here we are, all together. Me, the piece of shit white boy, and *mi prima*." He cocked his head and rested his hands on his hips. "Are you gonna tell him, cousin, or should I?" He grinned. "No? You want me to? Fine. I'll do the honors."

I looked from Tomas to her. "Tell me, Aurora."

"She doesn't have to tell you shit, white boy. You get that? I don't know who you think you are, coming into my territory, pissing all over my family like you're some kind of horny *perrito*."

"You don't own her," I said, my voice so low that it was almost a growl. "She can choose who she wants to be with."

I clenched my fists, tensed for a fight.

"Jesse. Tomas, Please!" She started to cry.

"Go ahead. Tell him!" He bounced on the balls of his feet. "No? No? Look," he said, glaring at me with that frozen grin plastered on his face. "Aurora's taken, okay? Engaged. To my homeboy Manuel, who just got out of jail yesterday." He wagged a finger in Aurora's face. "And if he found out that you've been slumming it with this, this *cucaracha*… Man, I don't know what he'll do to you."

"Don't let him bully you, Aurora."

Tears streamed down her cheeks, and she clutched his shirt. "Tomas, please," she begged, "Please don't tell him anything. Please. You're my cousin, I'm done with Jesse."

I felt the blood drain from my face.

"Aurora," I said in a lowered voice, "don't listen to him, he can't make you do what you don't want."

He shrugged her off and she stumbled to the ground. I helped her up.

"WHERE IS YOUR LOYALTY?" He punched the wall with his fist. "Who the fuck do you think you are? You belong to Manny. You belong to us."

I grabbed Aurora, and this time she let me hug her to my chest.

The kitchen staff finally noticed our shouting. The cooks came forward with arms outstretched.

Gary ran into the cafeteria toward us. He grabbed me and Tomas by the shoulders. "I thought you kids had learned your lesson last time," he said through clenched teeth. "I thought we were done with the fighting."

Tomas jerked out of Gary's grasp and moved toward the door. "Oh, we're done." He pointed a finger. "*Recuerda, Aurora. Lo que dijie.*"

"Come back here!" Gary shouted. The door banged shut. He cursed, flung it open and ran after Tomas.

I held Aurora up by the shoulders. "Don't cry," I whispered. "It'll be okay." I brushed my fingers under her chin and leaned in to kiss her.

She pulled away and wiped her red eyes. "It's not okay. You don't understand, do you? I'm pregnant."

She ran out the door.

* * *

The next day, I spent every free moment trying to find Aurora.

During rec, I spotted Guapa sitting on the worn couch, gossiping with all the other cholas. I walked up to her. "Where is she? I have to talk to her."

The girls exchanged glances. Finally Guapa lifted her head. "Look, she's in the Senior Girls' dorm. She's sick. She's with staff."

"Thanks," I said as I ran toward the door.

"Leave her be," Guapa called after me.

Boys were forbidden on that side of the Hall grounds. If one of us were caught there, it could mean loss of all privileges, or worse: solitary. But I didn't care. I had to see her.

I burst through the doors into the common area. A female counselor sat at the couch watching TV.

"Sampson," she said when she saw me. "Get out of here. You know the rules."

I scanned the rooms. "I have to — I have to talk with Aurora. Please."

She stood up, her hands on the walkie-talkie that she carried. "I am ordering you to leave, immediately." She pointed a finger toward the door. "Out."

"Rosa, it's okay." I heard the faint sound of Aurora's voice come from one of the sleeping areas. "Can I please just talk to him for a minute?"

Rosa glanced toward the door and hesitated. "Fine. I'll give you five minutes. But talk where I can see you. Hurry, I could get in serious trouble for this."

"Thanks." I ran to the room where I heard Aurora. She lay curled up on one of the beds. "Hey." I sat next to her. "What's going on?"

Her head rested on top of her hands. "I just don't feel good."

"Aurora?" I brushed her cheek with my fingers. "It's not true, is it? The baby?"

She closed her eyes. Her eyelids were shiny, as if she'd been crying for hours. "Yes."

"But, how? You don't look pregnant, and we never even — I mean, you know, nothing ever—"

"It's Manuel's."

She saw my eyes widen and raised her head from the bed. "From before, right before I got put in here." She smiled a strange smile. "You see? I told you—I'm bad. On the inside, I'm all rotten. It's better this way."

"No, you're not." I shook my head, trying to wrap my brain around it all. "I don't care that you're pregnant. I still love you."

"God, you're such a boy scout." Her laugh was short and strangled. "You don't understand, Jesse. He's out of jail now. I've been with him since I was thirteen years old. It's not like I can just walk away from him. We're from the same neighborhood. We have the same life."

I reached out and touched her arm. Her skin was golden and velvety, and I let my fingertips travel up her shoulder and to her neck, under the heavy fall of her hair. I pulled her neck forward, until our foreheads touched.

"Do you love him?" I asked in a low voice.

"Jesse."

"Do you?"

She looked down, tiny crystal teardrops clinging to her black eyelashes. "You know I don't."

Our lips were almost touching. "Then run away with me. I'll find a way. We'd live with my sister, and I could go to work. I'd help you raise your baby, Aurora. I love kids, I'm real good with them."

"I'm not keeping it."

I felt hollowness inside, like the first time I caught Mom shooting up. Or the time I found a dead baby bird on the ground, bits of shell clinging to its blue, unopened eyes.

My throat tightened. I pulled away to search her face. "Why?"

"Manuel already has two kids from other girlfriends. He said he doesn't want another baby to have to feed."

I stroked her hair. "He can't make you. It should be your choice, not his."

She didn't answer. I let a long silky strand of her hair pass between my fingers. "Aurora."

"You're too late," she whispered. "I already did it."

Twenty-One

```
shark (n): an active predator dangerous to
                    humans.
```

Aurora was gone in the morning. Nobody knew where she went. Some people said she escaped, and others said she was moved into a group home. Whatever the truth was, staff wouldn't say a word.

As for me, I walked around with a hollow pit in my stomach. Somehow, people knew to leave me alone. I couldn't sleep, I couldn't think, I couldn't eat.

The eating part—that was saying a lot.

When it was time for group, I told Lee I had a headache and he let me lay on my bed. I was almost out when Tim found me there.

"There you are." He jiggled my shoulder and I flicked my eyes open. "Come on, we're going to be late."

"I'm not going."

"Aw, please, you gotta go. It would be good to for you to talk about Aurora, anyway. Man, I know you gotta be hurting."

"I don't want to talk about her."

He gave a tentative smile. "Well, come for me, then. I want to tell everybody about what's going on. See, my grandmother's trying to get clearance for me from my social worker to go to my dad's memorial, but she doesn't think it's a good idea, so now we have to get a court order—"

"Look, Tim." I felt a red cloud build behind my eyes. "I don't really care, okay? I don't care about group, and I don't care about your stupid dad's memorial. What do you want to go there for, anyway? He was a pervert, a piece of shit, and he treated you like crap."

His face crumpled. "But I just thought… I thought that you'd want to hear…"

"You think too much, you know that? And your problems—man, Tim, you're a time suck. Grow up, and realize the truth. Your dad was messed up, and now you're messed up. End of story. Life's a frickin' sewer, and the sooner you realize that, the better off you'll be."

He stood up and took a step back from me. His eyes were wide. "Okay, Jesse. Okay. You know, you're right. I've been talking about myself too much, and I guess, I guess I'm sorry…"

He took off.

Shit. I was such an asshole. "Tim. Geez, come back. I'm just pissed off. Look, I'm sorry…*Tim*!"

I ran after him, but he was already gone.

*   *   *

During rec, I found Jaison playing basketball with Elliot and some other guys. "Anyone seen Tim?"

"Nope." Jaison spun around and shot the ball, it hit the rim and bounced off.

Elliot grabbed the ball, ducked under a tall red-headed kid, and dunked it, hanging off the hoop. "I just did." He wiped his face with his shirt and walked over to me. "He was with Tomas I think."

"What? Why?"

He shrugged. "I don't know. I think they were headed for the john."

I felt the hairs on my neck stand up as I raced over to the bathrooms. Just as I was about to push on the door, Tomas and Tim walked out. Tim looked at me with surprise.

"Jesse?"

"What are you doing here?"

Tomas hung his arm around Tim's neck with a thin smile on his lips. "What's the matter, can't Tim have other friends?"

I grabbed Tomas' shirt and pushed him against the wall. "Stay away from him. There's something wrong with you, you know that, Tomas? Even Aurora thought so."

He pushed me back with such force that I staggered back about four feet. "Yeah?" he said, brushing his shirt. "Well, who'd she listen to, then? Do you know where she is now? I know, *cabrón*, but do you?"

We stared at each other with pure hatred.

Tim tugged on my sleeve. "Come on Jesse," he said in a quiet voice, "let's go." He pulled me back. "Come on; don't get yourself in trouble again. It's not worth it."

I walked backward. "We're not done," I said to Tomas, pointing at his face.

He laughed. "Anytime, you name it." He lifted his chin. "Later, Timmy E."

*   *   *

The heat spell that started on Thursday lingered through the weekend.

It was especially hot that night. The swamp coolers weren't working so well, and everyone complained about trying to fall asleep in the relentless heat.

"Tim?" I heard him shift in his cot. "You awake?"

"Yeah."

"Are you still mad at me?" Tim hadn't been himself lately, and it got me worried. Maybe it was because of all the business with his dad's memorial, but still, I felt partly responsible. I swallowed. "For yelling at you yesterday? Look, you know I'm sorry. I've been messed up in the head lately. I shouldn't have said those things."

My skin was sticky with sweat.

"That's okay."

"I hope you get to go to your dad's memorial service."

"It already happened. It was today. The court said no, I couldn't go. It doesn't matter, anymore. You were right, anyway. I don't know why I care about him still."

"No, I was wrong. Just don't listen to me. I'm more screwed up than anybody."

"No, you're not." He turned to face me. "Jesse?"

"Mmm."

"I'm sorry about Aurora. That was messed up. Tomas is such an asshole. You didn't deserve that."

Neither did she, I thought.

But it got me thinking. Seemed to me, people like Tomas never did seem to get what was coming to them. It was the weaker ones, like my mom and Darryl and most of the kids around here that suffered from the system. People like Tomas seemed to rise to the top, like sharks, circling around the wounded.

"What were you doing yesterday, talking to him?"

"Oh, nothing."

He wasn't telling me the full story and we both knew it.

"Stay away from Tomas, Tim Em."

"I know. I do."

"That dude's a sociopath."

"Yeah." He chuckled. "He probably is."

"Whatever you were talking about, it probably wasn't good."

We were silent a long while when Tim's whispery voice cut through the hot air. "Thanks, Jesse."

I lifted my head from the pillow. "For what?"

"For being like a brother to me."

The corners of my mouth tugged. "Back at you, Tim. So, we're cool?"

"Yeah." His voice was soft, hardly there. "We're cool."

The heat of the night finally got to me. I closed my eyes and began to drift away. I was barely conscious when I heard him get up and head toward the bathroom.

Twenty-Two

gone (adj): 1. lost, ruined;
            2. not being there

The sound of Jaison screaming jarred me awake.

"Tim...Tim! What the fuck, man? Someone, anyone...help!"

I ripped off my sheets and raced to the bathroom. Tim was crumpled on the ground, a pile of vomit pooled beside him. In one frozen hand was a plastic baggie and in the other, a straw.

"Tim." I knelt beside him. His eyes were opened and brown powder dusted his nose.

"I woke up to pee and almost stepped on him. He's cold, Jesse. He's not moving, man." Jaison jiggled his leg. "Tim, wake up."

I slapped his cheeks. Despite the heat of the night they were like ice. "Wake up, Tim." Tears blurred my vision. "Quit messing with us. Wake up!"

Terry, the night counselor appeared at the door. "Oh, my God. Not again." He crouched down and felt for Tim's pulse on his neck, then grabbed his walkie-talkie. "Emergency, Senior Boys'. Red alert."

More guys crowded the doorway. "Is he dead?" Danny G asked. "Dude," he said, stepping forward. "Look at his eyes. They're all glassy."

Rage exploded inside of me. "Don't you talk about him." I jumped up and pinned Danny to the wall. "Don't you dare."

Out of the corner of my eye, I saw Tomas leaning against the far corner of the cottage, a small smile fixed on his punk ass face. Suddenly it all became clear. Tomas and Tim — when I saw them talking yesterday.

I released Danny G and darted over to Tomas, surprising him and knocking him to the floor.

"It was you!" My hands squeezed around his neck. "Yesterday. You gave him something." I banged his head against the linoleum. "You gave him something—just tell me, what was it?" My teeth were bared.

"Nothing he didn't want," he panted. We were locked in a death grip. Tomas' muscles shook as he pushed my jaw up with his palm. With his other hand he reached behind him and pulled something out of his pocket. "Nothing he didn't deserve. Now it's your turn."

He swung his arm back and shot toward my neck. I twisted when I saw a glint of metal. Moments later a blinding pain seared along my collarbone.

It looked like some type of homemade knife. I bent back his arm, breathing heavily. My blood dripped on top of his chest. I felt sick at the sight.

"You didn't—"

A bronze hand shot through and squeezed Tomas' wrist until it dropped to the floor. It was the Indian. I felt other hands grip me and pull me off of Tomas. The Indian straddled him, pinning him with his large frame.

My blood, slick and sticky, was everywhere.

"You fucking killed him, you psycho." I tried to lunge for him but the counselors held me back. "You did it."

By now Tomas was held by two security guards and the Indian. He spit in my direction.

"No, *puto*. He was upset because of you, homes. He told me you were mean to him." Tomas' eyes were tiny and feral, like the opossums that prowled the riverbanks back home.

I heard the creak of wheels and watched as the stretcher carrying Tim Emmett was wheeled through the dorm. One of his arms hung down. The place was now crowded with kids and staff and paramedics and cops. I watched as one of the paramedics covered his face with a sheet.

"No!" I cried. "Wake him up…you need to wake him up!"

Jaison's face was slick with tears.

"They've been working on him this whole time, Jesse. It's too late, he's gone."

*   *   *

I watched the moon rise through the small window of solitary. Its rays bathed the room in a gray sheen.

He was really gone.

Tomas was right. I had killed him. *If I had never said that stuff to him, he would have never got upset enough to score drugs off of Tomas. He'd still be alive.* I rolled over on my side.

Later that night, they had bandaged the wound on my collarbone with cotton and gauze.

"You got lucky this time," the nurse said as she cleaned the wound with antiseptic. "It's just a nick. If he got to your artery, you could have died too."

I didn't answer. It didn't matter, because at that moment I could care less whether I lived or died.

Staff decided I was a risk to others and myself, which is how I ended up in here. I was a risk to others. I ended up hurting everyone I cared for.

I closed my eyes. Everyone.

I couldn't get the image of Tim's frozen face as he lay in his own puke. Did it happen quickly, or did he feel pain? I saw the brown stuff on his nose. It looked like that cheap heroin that had been going around. Even Darryl stayed away from that stuff. I heard that you could get it for as little as ten bucks. If it came as a powder, you could snort it. The straw. That's what the straw was for.

The room got dark. I heard a sound and looked up. A shadow was at the window. I huddled in the corner of my bed. Tapping—it was unmistakable this time. I squinted closer and saw a face.

"Indian?" I whispered.

I could see his makeshift crowbar through the glass.

"I'm gonna pry it off," he said, his voice muffled. "Watch out in case the glass breaks." Within a minute he pulled off the pane of the window and poked his head in.

"What are you doing here?"

"The window just looks smaller than it really is. If you can get your head through, you can get out of here."

I blinked. "You're breaking me out?"

"It's what you wanted, isn't it?"

"Well, yeah. But, why now?"

His long hair hung down and he glanced behind him. "Look, we don't have much time. I'm leaving. You can either come with, or stay here."

My brain struggled to make sense of what he was saying. "No, wait. I'm in."

I walked over to the wall and realized I could barely touch the bottom of the window with my fingertips.

"You need to move the bed," he called. "If you stand up on the post you can reach it. You'll have to climb up."

As quietly as possible, I moved the bed over against the other wall. I climbed up and balanced my foot on the closest post. The metal of the windowsill felt cool against my palms.

The Indian leaned over and grabbed my forearms. I tensed my body for the jump.

"Ready?"

He nodded. "Go."

I jumped. My toes struggled to leverage against the crags in the wall as he strained to pull me up. With one final hoist, he leaned back.

We fell on top of the roof.

I heard the whir of the air-conditioning units and saw the tops of Senior and Junior Boys' dorms. A few lights were still on, and a police car was parked on the road.

"We'll be caught," I said, my breath catching.

"No way. It's the perfect time to split. The whole staff's distracted with Tim."

I rested my hands on my knees and caught my breath. "How

many times have you done that before?"

His face was as sober as always, but I thought I saw the beginning of a smile. "A few."

He motioned me over to the other side of the building. We half crawled, half crouched over to the side facing the main road. On the other side of the iron fence, a car idled with its lights off.

"Come on," he whispered.

We came to the lowest corner of the main building. The drop was about 12 feet.

The Indian peered over the edge. "We're going to have to jump. There's no other way."

"Let's do it."

He nodded once, crouched like a cat, and jumped. With a deep thud, I saw his body hit the grass and roll. He stood up and faced me.

"Your turn."

I jumped. When I fell, I hit my shoulder, and groaned. The bandaged wound still throbbed with pain. I looked up to see him tower over me.

He shook his head. "Clumsy white boy," he said, offering me a hand.

We ran over to the locked iron gate on the west end. The Indian pulled a set of keys out of his pocket. My mouth dropped. "Hey, where'd you get those?"

"Look." He turned the key in the lock, tossed the set on the grass and pushed me through the opening. "If we're going to hang together, we have to get some things straight." He slammed the gate closed.

"What's that?"

We ran toward the car. He opened the backseat door, and we both got in. The driver, an older man with thick gold earrings and eyeliner leaned back and gave him a kiss on the cheek.

The Indian turned and looked me dead in the eyes. "Don't ask questions. Don't be a pain in the ass. Deal?"

I watched as the Hall faded into the night.

"Deal," I said.

Twenty-Three

trick (n): a crafty procedure meant to deceive
or defraud.

The car sped away. And just like that, my life at the Hall turned into a bad memory. I settled in to my seat. The car, a late model silver Lexus, smelled like new leather and cigarettes.

"Jesse." The Indian tucked his hair behind his ears and nodded toward the front. "This here's my uncle, Toby."

Don't ask questions.

"Hi, Toby."

"Hi." He looked me over and his thin mouth curled up at the edges.

I cleared my throat and looked away. Tiny squares of red brake lights glowed around us, and beyond the cars, a sea of industrial buildings flanked by graffiti-stained concrete walls ran endlessly in each direction.

"Where are we going?" I asked. I caught myself when I saw the

Indian raise his eyebrows. "Ne—never mind."

"We're five minutes into it, and already you break one of my rules. Shit."

"Sorry." I grabbed my thighs to keep them from twitching. "A mistake."

And then he surprised me by breaking into a wide grin, the first time I saw him look any type of happy during the past ten weeks I knew him.

"You know, not many kids would have the cojónes to stand up to Tomas. Or jump that far."

His compliment made me feel hollow on the inside.

"No big deal."

Uncle Toby turned onto a freeway.

The Indian wiped his nose. "If it makes you feel any better, Tomas finally got a taste of his own medicine. They searched his room, found all kinds of contraband. Another knife, drugs, phone numbers." Uncle Toby passed him back a lit cigarette, and he took a quick drag. He cracked his window and blew the smoke out. "His ass is in juvie tonight," he said in a low, predatory voice.

"Oh."

It didn't make me feel any better. Tim Emmett — the only real friend I ever had — was dead, and it was because of me.

He took another deep drag and eyed me. "Don't do it," he said, shaking his head. "I know what you're thinking, and that shit is poison. It'll kill you, I know it will."

I bristled. "How do you know what I'm thinking?"

"I know." He grimaced. "You got that survivor's guilt written all over your face. Shit, you know how old Tim Em was when he first got to the Hall?"

I shook my head.

"Seven. I know, because I was there too, by then. I was ten."

"So?"

His eyes glinted. "You know how many times that kid's tried to commit suicide? The first time was when he was like, nine. Tried to light himself on fire."

Like his dad did.

"My point, Jesse, is that Tim was bound to do it. It was just a matter of time. And as much as you want to blame Tomas, or yourself, or the system or whatever, you can't. Because he did it to himself."

It was the most I'd ever heard the Indian talk during the whole time I'd known him. But I didn't want him talking about Tim, and suddenly the sound of his voice and the greasy nicotine stench of the car made me feel sick.

I scooted over to the edge of the seat and blinked the burning tears away. "Let's drop it." I grasped the door handle tightly in my knuckles.

After a while the Indian cleared his throat. "Don't you want to know where we're going?"

"Sure. Yeah."

"Truckston."

I snapped my head up in surprise. "You're taking me to Truckston?"

He looked pleased with himself. "That's where you're from, right?"

"Right."

"So that's where we're going. I have to do a little job over there, and I figured I could bring you along. Then you can see that sister you always talk about. What do you call her?"

"Pony."

I felt a stab of guilt as I said her name. With all the Tim Em stuff, I hadn't thought about her at all. It didn't matter now, because what he was offering was more than I dared to hope for — an actual ride back home. No drug muling, no hitchhiking, no walking unknown streets in the dark.

"Thanks, man." I felt the lump form in my throat. "I owe you one."

He stubbed the cigarette out and tossed it through the crack, the orange embers spinning onto the asphalt.

"Don't mention it," he said.

*   *   *

The clock on the dashboard read 3:00 am. We got off at an exit that said Pasadena. I vaguely remembered watching the Rose Bowl parade on TV with Darryl, and it was in Pasadena.

Uncle Toby drove through a downtown area until we pulled up alongside a high-rise. *Easy Condo Living* the sign said. *Close to the Freeway. Call 555-2929 for Your Free Tour.* The car idled.

The Indian flared his nostrils. "I thought I was dropping you off at your place," he said.

Uncle Toby kept his hands on the steering wheel. "You have to do me a little favor first." A muscle moved in his jaw. "So does he."

The Indian pounded a fist on the back of the seat. "No. No way. This wasn't part of the deal."

"You're not really in a position to make deals now, are you?"

"Shut up." There was a shakiness in his voice.

"You're doing what I tell you to do. Because that's the way it goes, isn't it?" He reached out a hand to stroke the Indian's cheek.

He flinched.

"I did you both a big favor tonight; you can do this little one for me."

Silence.

Uncle Toby's voice turned into a croon. "Come on. I owe this guy."

"What's going on?" I asked, trying to catch the Indian's eye. "Hey. Indian —what's going *on*?"

He ignored me.

"Fine," he said after a long, hard pause. "But not him."

Uncle Toby looked me over with a tiny smile. "But he looks so fresh. And he pays double for two."

The Indian clenched his fists. "No."

Uncle Toby's voice dropped an octave, a warning sound. "Maybe I'm not asking… Maybe he's already expecting two."

"No!" In an instant, the Indian was across the console, his hands around Uncle Toby's throat. "You touch him, Toby, and the deal's off. The *whole* deal. Got it? Not a hair." His face was tight, contorted with rage as he squeezed the older man's neck until his entire face turned a deep, throbbing purple.

"Indian!" I heard someone scream, and it was a couple seconds before I realized that the voice was mine. Before a thought could form in my head, I had opened the door and found myself running down the street.

"Jesse!" I heard the Indian come after me, but my legs wouldn't stop even if I wanted them too. He caught up to me and grabbed me by the shoulder, causing me to lose my balance and fall sideways.

I scrambled up on my knees. "Just stay away from me," I said, panting.

"Please," he begged in a ragged voice. "Please don't go. He won't hurt you, I promise."

I looked back to the car, which still hummed in park down the way. "Let's just go," I said quietly. "Right now. We can outrun him."

His eyes had a hollowed, desperate expression. "No. No — you don't understand Toby. I *have* to do it…" His voice trailed off. "It's just part of it, is all. Besides, we need money for the trip."

He started backing up toward the apartments. "Please stay — will you stay? I'll be right back."

As he neared the apartment, Uncle Toby rolled down the window and called out, "It's 314-B. Third floor."

The Indian strode to the building, his long hair swinging loose behind him. "I know," he muttered.

The first beam of sunlight snuck out over the treetops and shone in my eyes. I stood there, frozen, as if in a dream. Every fiber of my being wanted to bolt, to run and never look back.

But if I did…

The Indian said he'd take me to Truckston. I decided to wait an hour.

The window rolled down again and Uncle Toby hung his head out. "Hey, kid —you want to come in?"

"I'm fine out here."

"I won't touch you — not unless you want me to." He laughed, a low, chortling sound that turned my insides to glue.

I glared at him.

"Geez." Uncle Toby rolled his buggy eyes. "Touchy."

I leaned against the hood of the car, nodding off from time to time. I could hear Uncle Toby fiddling with the radio stations and the sounds of the morning traffic as the very early risers headed to work.

I kept my eyes closed, trying to shut everything else out.

*   *   *

It was getting light by the time the Indian retuned. He flung open the door and climbed in the back.

Uncle Toby sat in the front seat and started the car. "See, that wasn't so hard, was it?"

"Just shut up." The Indian hugged his arms to his chest.

"Gimme, gimme." Uncle Toby snaked his arm behind the backseat and snapped his fingers.

The Indian pulled out a wad of cash and counted. He pressed half of the bills into his hand. "That's the last time," he said quietly.

"You always say that."

"Well this time, I mean it."

"Whatever you say."

The tone in Uncle Toby's voice gave me the chills. I kept my eyes on the scenery. I was almost sixteen, but I felt old, like I'd already lived a million years. Even my bones ached.

We drove to a tree-lined neighborhood with small houses and tidy lawns. Uncle Toby parked in front of one and handed the Indian a piece of paper.

"Here's the address," he said. "And here's an extra phone. Call me when you've made the handoff."

"Yeah."

Uncle Toby got out of the car and the Indian moved up front. He motioned for me to follow.

"Drive safely," said Uncle Toby, with a wink. "Hurry home." He leaned into the car and tried to give the Indian a kiss. He shirked away, a scowl on his face. "You'll forgive me," he said, as he walked toward the house. "You always do."

The Indian gunned the gas and we went peeling down the small street.

"Go fuck yourself," he whispered under his breath.

I smelled the burnt rubber of the wheels beneath us.

Twenty-Four

getaway car (n): a motor vehicle, used to flee
the scene of a crime.

We drove for a few hours through the Grapevine without speaking a word. I think I was still in shock. Tim Emmett hadn't even been dead more than a few hours. I should have been glad that I was, finally, really making my way back to Truckston, but all I could taste was the bile way back in my throat.

"Do I make you sick?" We passed craggy mountains as Indian's voice cut through the silence.

"No, man." His question caught me off guard. I cleared my throat. "No way."

"Huh." There was a long pause. "Well, I make myself sick."

"Hey. It's cool."

"My mom sold herself for as long as I can remember. Toby was my mom's boyfriend."

I stole a look at him. "I get it."

"It's a living." He jutted his jaw out and flexed his fingers on the steering wheel. They were long and delicate, like this girl's I once knew who played piano. "This car's stolen, just in case you're wondering. Toby's got a lot of... side businesses."

I pressed my lips together. "You're giving me a ride. That's all I need to know."

I felt weird inside, felt like if I opened my mouth too much, that everything inside would come rushing out, and wouldn't stop. Like Tim had said at group that one time —an eruption that would just keep flowing and flowing. But part of me knew that I needed to stuff everything away, in order to keep going.

I didn't want to know about the Indian, about his mom selling her body or how he's sick of what he does with Toby. All I focused on was the fact that every mile we drove put me closer back to my old life, put me closer to Pony.

His eyes stayed focused on the road and I was grateful for the silence. I pulled the picture of Aurora out of my back pocket and slowly unfolded it. The creases were deep, and the pencil smudges covered the paper in gray.

Where was she? I wondered again. Did she go back to Manuel? Did she even miss me?

The Indian looked deep in thought as he kept a tight grip on the wheel. The humming sound of the engine had almost put me to sleep when he cleared his throat. "You should know, I'm leaving him," he said.

"What?"

"He thinks I'm taking the car to Truckston, to his friend who owns a chop shop. What he doesn't know is that after I drop you off, I'm gone."

"Where're you headed?"

"My grandfather is Havasupai," he said, his eyes softening at the corners. "He lives on the rez in Arizona. I used to visit there when I was little. I'm going to look him up, and see if he'll let me stay. Start a new life, turn a new leaf, and all that shit." He cracked a small smile.

"So it's true, then. You really are an Indian?"

He nodded. "Almost 25 percent."

"But what's your name? It can't be Indian."

The corners of his mouth tugged. "Walter." He said it so low that I could barely hear him. "Walter Blackfoot."

"Well, thanks, Walter," I said. "Thanks — for everything."

We got into Truckston around ten in the morning. We were so tired that we pulled the car into a deserted parking lot and slept with the seats reclined. When we woke up, it was already evening, so we ate at the McDonald's close by.

"So what's your plan?" Walter asked, his mouth full of burger. "To find your sister?"

"Plan?" I didn't really have a plan. I hadn't thought that part out, yet. "I don't know." I took a swig of Coke. "I guess I'll go by the CPS office and turn myself in, see if they'll place me with Pony."

Walter threw his head back and laughed. "God, you kill me. You are so *green*, you know that? I knew you lived out in the country, but shit, you are completely backwater." He cocked his head. "Turn yourself in? Seriously, man."

I felt my jaw clench. "Do you have a better option?"

"Actually, I do." He leaned in, his eyes locked in on mine. "Come with me. Let's get your sister, and take her with us."

I heard my heart beating like a drum in my ears. "Seriously?"

I stumbled on my words. "Like — like...*kidnapping*?"

He leaned closer to me until I could see my face reflecting in his pupils. "How can it be kidnapping if she's your sister?"

I couldn't argue with him there.

"You said your mom's in jail, right?"

"Well, yeah."

"Locked up — she'll do time?"

The last time the social worker came she said my mom was in for three to five years. I'd probably be eighteen by the time she got out.

"Yeah," I whispered.

"Your sister — look, there's no guarantees. I have three brothers, somewhere. Each and every one of them have been adopted. *Adopted.* I don't even know where they live. There's no telling if they place you with her, or ship you off somewhere else."

I had heard the horror stories and had laid in bed many nights in the Hall worrying about that. Back then, all I could focus on was getting here, being closer to her. But now that I was actually here, I realized I didn't have a clue about what to do next. Walter's plan didn't sound half bad.

"What would we do in Arizona?"

"We could work, in a motel or as guides, for the tourists." His eyes grew wistful. "My grandfather has horses that he rents out. The Havasupai own the back entrance to the Grand Canyon. There are falls there, they're famous—the most beautiful thing you've ever seen in your whole life. The water is so clear, that you can see the fish swimming at the bottom."

I loved any type of water, and Pony was obsessed with horses— the plastic kinds. She would die if she ever had the chance to actually ride a real one.

"You're forgetting one important thing. I don't even know where she is. She could be anywhere. How do you figure we'll find that out?"

He shook the ice in his cup. "That, my friend, you can just leave up to me. Trust me," he said with a sober grin. "I know people."

*   *   *

We slept a few more hours in the car, until it was fully dark.

Walter drove to the eastside, my old neighborhood, and pulled up alongside of a seedy roadside bar: The Stray Dog.

"Hey, I can't hang here too long," I said, eyeing the ragged people filtering in. Darryl and Mom spent many a Friday night here, and it wasn't uncommon for Beto to toss back a few cold ones either. I felt my neck grow clammy. "This is close to my old neighborhood, and I sort of made some enemies before I split."

"Relax." He grinned, as he stepped out of the car. "You worry too much. I know this guy — a business associate." he added, when he saw my raised eyebrows. "I think he can help. He was a narc for the Sheriff a while back, and he can find just about anything out."

I slouched down in my seat. "I'm gonna stay in the car, Walter. I don't like being back here. Just—just hurry."

I peeked up over the dashboard. Walter flashed his fake ID to the bouncer and walked inside.

The windows were cracked. The scent of pot mixed with the hot summer breeze as it kicked up trash through the dirt parking lot. Still, I could smell the familiar tang of the wild sage that grew alongside of the river. It smelled of home.

After a long hour, the door opened.

I saw Walter exit with two other figures. He walked over.

"Come on out," he said. "I want you to meet Murray." I climbed out of the car, and stood in the shadows.

A big truck-driver-looking guy with beefy arms and a balding Mohawk pumped my arm. "Pleasure," he said. "You need to find someone, a sister? No sweat. We can find her, piece of cake. We'll need her name, age, description. But if we're able to get the information you want, we need to agree on a payment."

"Uh…" I dropped my eyes. "I don't really—"

"We'll get you covered, don't worry about it." Walter flashed me a warning look. "Let's discuss price after we get the info. I work with Toby. You know I'm good for it."

Murray caressed the hood of the Lexus. "So after all this, I get the car?"

Now things started to make sense. Murray must be the one who ran the chop stop. Knowing that in the end, we were stiffing him out of the car made me nervous.

Real nervous.

"For sure, bro." He clapped Murray on the back. At almost eighteen years old, he was the ultimate con artist.

I swallowed.

I was way out of my league.

"Let me introduce you to my new business partner," Murray said. "Yo." He craned his neck toward the guy standing behind him. "Come and meet… *hey!*" He thwacked him in the head. "What in the hell are you doing? Quit smoking that shit. It kills your brain cells, Merlin."

He pulled him forward, into the light. Merlin looked up from the bong he was sucking on and we locked eyes.

Holy freaking crap.

"Walter?" My voice was thin and strangled as I backed up. "We need to go." I flung open the car door and scrambled in, locking it behind me.

Merlin missed me by a hair and began pounding on the glass. "Open the door, Jesse! Fucking punk-ass loser! *Thief*! You owe me... I'm telling Beto you're here!"

Walter was hot behind me. He jumped in the car, turned on the engine, and gunned it in reverse. "What the hell was that?"

I buckled my seat belt. "Just go. I'll tell you later," I panted. "Go."

Merlin was still alongside of us, pounding away. "You see this, Jesse?" He pointed to his face, where an angry red scar ran jagged across his cheek. "My payment from Beto for you losing his drugs. I'm coming to find your sorry ass. You owe me. Jesse!"

I clutched the armrests with white knuckles. "Faster," I whispered.

Walter backed out of the parking lot, rammed the car into forward, and raced onto the freeway. I could see Merlin in the rearview mirror, flipping us off. Murray threw up his hands in exasperation.

Walter cocked an eyebrow at me as he sped down the 178. "I'm thinking that maybe you're not as green as I thought," he said with a wry grin.

"Just drive," I said. "And don't kill us."

"We're going to have to skip out on your sister, you realize that." Walter swerved around a Yukon with the words Soccer Mom splayed on the bumper.

My head squeezed with pressure. "No!" I said. "No, don't you dare. We can't leave her here, you promised me, Walter."

He shook his head. "We need to leave town now. You could get yourself killed by those guys." He wove in between two more cars. A horn blared behind us.

"Crap!"

Walter clutched the steering wheel and floored the gas. "They could be following us right now."

I looked in the rearview mirror. "I don't see anyone following—-"

Sirens.

Behind us, on the left hand-side, a cop car snaked out from behind a billboard. The familiar blare of a siren screamed behind us.

"Oh, my God."

"Shit." His lips thinned. "Hold on." He cranked the wheel a hard right and turned off on a dirt road that led to a sea of orange orchards. "Listen," he said, "There's a back way through the mountains. If I floor it to the bridge, we can make it." The car jostled and I braced myself as we sped through the dense trees. Clumps of branches and oranges fell like hail against the window shield.

I clutched the door handle with both hands. "No. Please, just let me out here. Please, Walter."

He shook his head. "You'll be caught, you know that."

The sirens were close behind us.

"Please, let me off! I'll take my chances, you gotta understand. Havasupai. Arizona. I'll get her and come find you."

Droplets of sweat ran down the side of his face. "Fine. Have it your way." He took one last look at me. "When I say run, you run. Got it?"

"Okay." I tensed against the door.

He spun the car down another row and slammed on the brakes.

"Go. Hide; I'll try to lead them off your trail."

In that split second, I was motionless.

Walter leaned over and yanked open my door. "Go, goddammit! GO!" He pushed me into the open air.

I stumbled out of the car, and ran down an empty row. I saw the Lexus speed up the rest of the hill, with two cop cars now close behind.

Keeping close to the trees for cover, I ran down the last row. If I could make it to the river, I'd be safe. It was just a half a mile, maybe less away.

I looked to the right, then to the left. When I was certain no one was around, I fled the safety of the orchard toward the north, where the river snaked through, into the wide open.

"Halt! Police!" Several pairs of footsteps clustered behind me. "We got him."

I dropped my chin to my chest.

"Put your hands on your head. Now!"

I did as the voice said and heard the footsteps shuffle closer.

Facing me were three cops with their weapons drawn and pointed right at me.

"You have the right to remain silent. Anything you can and will say will be held against you in a court of law..."

Twenty-Five

juvie (n): a youth detention center, also known
as juvenile hall, for young people, often
termed juvenile delinquents.

The food was better in juvie. Eggs and bacon for breakfast, lasagna for lunch, some type of chickeny-lemony-rice thingy for dinner. Cheesecake that they served in tiny little squares with bright red congealed cherries on top. Kool-Aid and water to drink, even two snacks.

Man, I couldn't complain about the food.

Actually, the kids weren't too bad, either. They were just like the kids at Emerson, some a little rougher, some not so much.

But I kept to myself. It was weird, it was like they knew not to mess with me. Which was good, because I wasn't in the mood to be messed with. At all.

I had been locked up for a month when the judge decided to let me go. Insubstantial evidence, my court-appointed lawyer explained to me. *Insubstantial*, because there was no *evidence*. There was no Lexus, or Indian for that matter.

He got away, I found out. Escaped the cops, evaded arrest. Got away. Somehow the thought of the Indian free, swimming with his grandpa in the clear blue waters of the Havasupai Falls made it not matter so much that I was the one who got caught.

On the day of my release, they called for me during PE. I was doing push-ups with the rest of the inmates in the main yard. Sixty minutes of straight exercises — old-school style. It felt good to sweat, and when my heart beat hard it reminded me that I was still alive. My muscles had grown strong and lean in the past thirty days and no one could ever accuse me of being skinny anymore.

"Sampson." Forty-six, forty-seven, forty-eight, forty-nine, *fifty*. After the last push-up, I lifted my head. A juvenile correctional officer stood over to the side. He crossed his arms. "It's time. You ready?"

My heart throbbed steadily as I wiped the sweat off of my brow. "As ready as I'll ever be."

*   *   *

I felt numb as he escorted me down the long, concrete hall toward the discharge area. When he opened the door, a large Mexican guy stood up.

"Hey, Jesse." He smiled and offered me his hand. "Wow. You've gotten big."

I studied him. He kind of looked like a panda bear, with bright, black eyes, curly hair, and a beard. "Do we know each other?"

"It sure has been a long time. Do you remember me?"

I squinted. "Nope." There was something sorta familiar about his face, but I couldn't place it. Then I saw the yellow file sitting on the table, the badge hanging from a lariat around his neck. "Oh. Are you my social worker?"

When he smiled his eyes almost disappeared into the folds of fat. "I am. But, I remember you from years ago. Gosh, you were just a little kid back then, like six or something. My desk was across from Mandy's."

The memories snapped me back to over ten years ago. The pretty young social worker who was nice to me the night they first took me away from my mom. I could almost smell the sugary scent of her perfume. It had been such a long time, but I felt as if it just happened.

"You had crayons in your desk. And candy."

"That's right."

"Theo?" I guessed.

"Yeah." He nodded. "Theo Morales. And I still have crayons in my desk, if you ever want them."

"Mandy. Is she still there, working?"

"No. She left years ago. I think she has three kids now, she stays at home with them."

"Oh." I wondered if she remembered me. *Probably not*, I thought bitterly, and shook the thought away. "So what now? Am I back in the system?"

He chuckled. "I'm afraid you are. Sorry 'bout that. I know that you were trying to run away from Emerson before you got put in here. But we can't just let you roam around free now, can we? Since you're been released from juvenile hall, you are back in our custody.

Child Protective Services."

CPS—the whole reason I escaped the trailer home from the drug raid in the first place. If I had just stayed put, I would have been with Pony, and wouldn't have gotten tangled up in all the crap I had been the last several months.

I glanced at that yellow folder, knowing it contained a whole boatload of information about me—my prior time in foster care, info about my mom's arrest, and where Pony was. "Have you seen her?"

"Who, son?"

"Pony. Is she okay?"

"Pony?" Theo looked momentarily confused.

"My sister."

"Oh, yes." He consulted his folder. "You mean Crystal. Crystal Garreth." He shot me a contrite look. "You must forgive me, I was just assigned your case a couple days ago and I've got over seventy kids in my caseload. But yes, of course, I have seen Crystal. And yes, I can confirm that she's here."

"She's in foster care?"

"Yes."

"And she's safe?" I exhaled impatiently. "She's okay?"

His face softened. "She's okay, Jesse."

"So what now? Am I being placed with her?"

The twinkle in his eyes faded. "I wish it were that easy. Most people aren't comfortable taking in someone so old, with the, uh, history you've had."

It's what the social worker back at Emerson said. *A history.* Now I had a history, whatever the hell that meant.

"Where am I going, then?"

"I have to put you in a temporary placement, Jesse," he said in a soft voice. "Just for a couple of months, hopefully. But the good news is, I have you on the list for a couple really great group homes. There's one out in the mountains just a few hours from here that has horses, and teaches you vocational skills. I think you might really like it."

I heard horror stories about group homes back at the Hall. The fights, the drugs, the counselors who came in and out, punching the clock every eight hours. But a part of me wondered if it even mattered. Aurora had said something like that the night we first met — same old shit, inside or outside. So far, I was beginning to think she was right.

"Jesse." He waved his hand across my face. "Earth to Jesse. Are you here?"

"What if I don't want to go into a group home? What if I just… won't go?"

He shifted his gaze to the armed officer standing by the front window to the visitation room and lowered his voice. "Son, don't do this. It's not worth it, trust me. You'll end right back up in this pit and you wouldn't want that, would you? Come on now, let's get into my car, I'll buy you a burger, and we can talk about it on the way."

"Can I at least see her?"

He brightened. "Of course you can. Once we get you settled, we'll arrange a visit right away. How would you like that?"

I lifted my chin. "How would I *like* that? Do I even have a choice?"

He couldn't answer me.

Twenty-Six

foster family (n): a temporary home.

We drove about five miles out of town, on the west side. "The De Leons are a new foster family," Theo said as we passed empty fields and long, ranch style homes. Though it was already October, it was still warm, the early-evening sky deepening into a deep, cerulean blue.

"They're both teachers, so that's nice, right? They're waiting to adopt, but they want a child under five years."

I looked out the window, bored with his constant banter. "Just tell me when I get to see my sister. I want to see her."

"Yeah." His belly spilled out over the seat belt, and he leaned back in his seat as he drove. "Okay. I'll work on it. When you get settled, we can arrange a visit."

I looked out the window. The west side. I had never been on this side of town before, and it was sort of in the country. Lots of homes had barns, and horses, and wide-open fields. In between the houses, tumbleweeds caught along the barbed wire fences.

We pulled up alongside of a scrubby ranch-style home similar to all the other ones we passed. Five junkers sat on cinderblocks in the driveway, and a cluster of chickens pecked at the scrubby weeds in the front yard.

I took it all in. "This place looks like a dump."

"Jesse." Theo shot me a pleading look. "I'm begging you, here. For old time's sake, promise me one thing."

"I didn't know we had old times."

"Please. You don't have a lot of options. Give this place a chance, will ya?"

I got out of the car, slammed the door behind me, and headed toward the front door. A scabby chicken dodged my path and with every step, I felt a sense of dread.

Foster care.

I was going back into foster care.

Theo waddled behind me, mopping his face with a handkerchief. He reached over and knocked.

An olive-skinned guy, with tubed earplugs and dreads opened the door. "Hey, Theo," the guy said in a soft voice. He looked about as opposite of a foster parent as I could possibly imagine. I tried to conceal my surprise. He reached over and pumped Theo's hand. "How's it going?" He wore a Bob Marley T-shirt and thrashed Birkenstocks. Intricate tattoo sleeves covered both arms.

Theo hugged that damned yellow file close to his chest. "Good, good, Daniel. Great to see you." His eyes were overly bright, and he clapped me hard on the shoulder. "This is Jesse Sampson. Jesse," he said to me as if I were his show-and-tell. "Can you say hi?"

"Hey." I kept my arms crossed tightly against me.

"Welcome, Jesse. I'm Daniel De Leon."

I looked him up and down. Most of them were fat, old, and in it for the money. Or other things, I thought with disgust. "You're a foster parent?"

"What do you say, Theo? Am I a foster parent?" He laughed. "I guess I am. You'll be my first foster kid, though. Maybe you could help explain things to me. Show me the ropes."

"It's not rocket science."

He smiled, ignoring my comment, and looked over at the car. "So, should we get the rest of your stuff?"

"No."

He raised his eyebrows. "Huh?"

"I have *no stuff.*"

Theo stroked his beard. "Well, this is all he has for now, unfortunately. He didn't take anything with him when he left Emerson Hall—right Jesse? And he didn't have anything when he was inventoried at juvie."

"Yeah," I added. "At juvie."

"Oh, no problem." He smiled. "I think we can handle getting you some new clothes. Actually I think my wife might be picking some stuff up right now."

I shrugged. "Whatever."

We walked inside and sat at the kitchen table. After they signed a bunch of paperwork, Theo turned to leave.

"I think this will work out just fine." Theo just stood there looking like someone shoved sunshine up his ass and grinned to no one in particular. I was beginning to think he had a mental problem. "Don't you?"

I bent closer to him. "How long do I have to be here?" I asked, under my breath.

"Just a couple of months. Maybe less, hopefully." He opened the front door. "We'll be in touch, Jesse."

The door closed behind him with a *thunk*. I had the irrational impulse to run after him.

I closed my eyes and breathed. *You can do this.*

"Well, now," Daniel said with a smile. "Come one. Let's show you around." He motioned for me to follow him. The guy limped when he walked, and had the slow, unhurried gait of someone who wasn't in the rush to get anywhere. I bet the guy smoked a lot of pot. *Probably a lot more*, I decided. With his long, waist-length dreads and deep-set eyes, he definitely had that look about him.

How could they even have let this guy take care of kids?

The house was cluttered, with worn furniture and holes in the carpet. Lots of little spidery plants hung from pots, and dozens of books crammed into the bookshelf by the fireplace. He picked up a newspaper left on the ground and hastily folded it up. "I guess it's not much," he said, "but it works for us."

He showed me the backyard, which was filled with more diseased chickens and a mangy-looking garden. The rest of the lawn was filled with waist-high weeds. Back inside, we walked down the hall and passed a closed door. I followed him into a bedroom.

"Here's where you'll sleep." The room was decorated as a nursery, with a crib and train wallpaper. A twin bed with a train quilt was wedged in one corner with a big stuffed bear resting on top. "Sorry about the room," he said with an embarrassed smile. "It's a little young. I guess Bethany sort of got caught up in the whole adoption idea."

Trains. The room was decorated with trains.

A memory, dark and suffocating, and one that I never remembered before, rose to the surface like an oil slick on water.

When I was eight, my room had trains.

Pressure tightened itself around my chest and I steadied myself on the bedpost as the big splotches, amoeba-like, started to form behind my eyes.

"Jesse, are you okay?" He placed a hand on my back.

I shirked it off. "Just — I'm fine." I took a couple of deep breaths, trying to regain my composure, trying push away the images that invaded my brain. "I'm fine. Look, it's been a long day," I said. My voice sounded to me as if it was underwater. "If you don't mind, I think I'm going to turn-in early."

"Oh." He looked disappointed. "Okay. But you haven't met Bethany yet, and we have lasagna cooking in the oven. Don't you like lasagna?"

"Not really hungry." I shook my head even as my stomach growled in protest. "It's just been a really long day. No offense."

His eyebrows knit together. "Do you get panic attacks? Maybe I should call Theo or someone—"

"I said no!" My hand was shaking as I gripped the bedpost.

"Fine," he said, his eyes staying on me. "But if you change your mind, we'll leave a plate for you in the oven." He slowly backed out of the room and closed the door.

I threw the big teddy bear off the bed and lay down on the quilt. My hands were still shaking as I slid them down my face. I reached into my back pocket and pulled out a folded paper and carefully opened it up. I smoothed it out and looked at her face. Aurora — the picture I drew for her, the picture she gave back to me. Did she already know back then that she was going to leave?

Wherever she was, did she think about me at all?

Only a few months. I'd be here only a few months before there was room at that group home.

But then what?

It was just a matter of time before Merlin and Beto found me, and when they did, it would all be over.

That kneading, tugging sensation spread through my gut, when I remembered Merlin's face as we sped away. "*I'm telling Beto you're here,*" he screamed. Something told me that they were still looking for me, and when they did, it would be all over.

I needed a plan, fast.

*   *   *

I was suffocating, drowning, deep under the surface, struggling, gasping to breathe. The room closed in around me, and everywhere I felt hands, arms, restraining me. And in my mouth, my nose, clinging to my skin, creeping down my torso, everywhere the sickly sweet scent of black licorice...

The hands in my dream shook me, and when I looked up, I saw him standing over me, tall and looming and dark. I screamed, and I tried to get away, as far away as possible. I ran, and found myself falling, falling backward.

"Don't touch me! Don't touch me!"

"Bethany — help me, turn on that light. Jesse! Jesse, wake up. You're dreaming — you're having a nightmare."

"What?" The room lit up and I opened my eyes, squinting

against the glare and bleary with sleep. My mind worked to make sense of where I was — my room? The Hall? Juvie? I looked around, and after a few moments I realized where I was, I was in the foster home, and it was Daniel who stood above me, shaking me awake.

"Jesse, hey, it's okay." He was crouched down beside me, and it was then that I realized I was on the ground, the sheets in a sweaty tangle around me.

I got up, still groggy, my pulse still rapid and pounding in my ears. "You can go now — I'm fine." I looked up and saw a woman in a purple bathrobe standing by my doorway with a worried expression.

"Here." Daniel put an arm around me as if to help me back into bed.

"Don't touch me!" The adrenaline, a current moving just below the surface, surged back, breaking through my skin. "Please — I got it." I saw them exchange a glance. "Okay? I got it."

Twenty-Seven

comfortable: (n) easy.

The crow of a rooster woke me up. When I finally opened my eyes, the clock on the wall read 11:00 am. Eleven. Really? Did I really sleep that long?

When I saw the sheets crumpled in a puddle down by my legs, the teddy bear tossed into the center of the room, dimly, the memory of the night before slowly surfaced back to me.

I could leave. Run away. Maybe I *should* just leave. It would be easy enough to do — there were no walls to keep me in around here. It would be easy enough to find Walter, make my way to Arizona and start a new life. I'd never been out of California, never been anywhere but my summer at the Hall, but I could find him, I knew I could.

But I knew I couldn't. I couldn't leave Pony.

*   *   *

I got up and creaked open the door. The place sounded like it was empty.

Would they have left me alone on my first day? Maybe last night freaked them out and Theo was on his way to get me right now, I thought.

I found the kitchen and saw a plate on the counter — pancakes and eggs covered in cellophane. The plate was still warm, and a note on top read: *Help yourself to the microwave.*

I inhaled the food and opened the fridge, looking for more. Full of food, I couldn't believe it. Yogurts, juice, cheese, all types of salad dressing. Is this how regular people lived? I found my dinner plate from last night, and ripped off the cellophane. Standing with the fridge wide open, I ate the lasagna right there with my hands, then washed everything down with a long, deep chug of milk, straight from the carton.

"There you are." The back door opened, and the woman from last night walked through, carrying a basket of eggs. "I was wondering when you'd finally wake up."

"Sorry," I said quickly and wiped my mouth.

"Oh, please. I have three brothers—drinking from the carton is practically encoded into your DNA," she said with a laugh.

"Thanks for the breakfast."

"Oh, sure—you got enough?" I nodded. "Good. Well, I'm Bethany." She gave me a quick hug, and stepped away. She wore overalls and her curly hair was tied back with a bandanna. "We didn't get a chance to really meet last night." Her eyes crinkled when she smiled. "How are you doing?"

"I'm fine."

"Hmm." She tilted her head in a quick, birdlike manner.

"Seemed like you had a hard time, last night."

"No." I felt my face flush. "Just a bad dream. That's all — I get them all the time. Sorry if it freaked you guys out."

"It didn't freak us out. We were just worried about you."

"No need to worry."

"It must have been pretty traumatic—all that you've been through." She opened the fridge and began placing the eggs inside. "It's a lot for a kid like you to process."

"Never better." I stood there fidgeting as I watched her put the eggs away. "What are you doing home? I thought you worked."

"I do — I'm leaving in a minute." A tiny crystal sparkled from her nose as she smiled. She was young — even younger than Daniel — in her early twenties at most, I figured. "But we don't want to leave you alone on your first day, now, do we? Daniel just got back from his weekly meeting, so I'll leave in a few. He'll get you settled."

"Meeting?"

"AA — he gets real cranky when he misses. Daniel's funny that way. Come on," she said, leading me down the hall. "He's in our hobby room."

"Doesn't he work, too?"

"He teaches Special-Ed, but he took the day off. For you."

We walked into the room next to mine that had been closed yesterday. Daniel sat at a chair restringing a guitar. "Oh, hey Beth… morning, Jesse," he said. "I didn't hear you get up."

"I didn't mean to sleep so long."

Five more guitars hung on one wall, and on the opposite wall, an easel sat in the corner, with an unfinished portrait of an older woman tilted against it.

I eyed the portrait. Whoever was painting it had some definite talent. The colors were vibrant, bold, and the use of shading was impeccable. I took a step closer. "Are these acrylics?"

"Yes, they are." Bethany tilted her head in a quick, birdlike fashion. "Are you an artist?"

"Oh, no," I answered swiftly. That was another lifetime ago. I could never imagine painting again after Aurora, and I felt a flash of pain as I thought of her. "It's good, though."

"I could teach you," she said. "That's what I do—I teach art at Central High, it's where you'll be going."

"School?" My mind struggled to wrap itself around the word.

Daniel cleared his throat. "Well, yeah — Theo said to register you today. You're a junior, right?"

I guess technically it was my junior year but I hadn't even thought about school. We had to go to class in juvie, but that was such a joke it hardly counted. Here it was, already October, and I had some type of dim recollection that school was going on for other kids my age, but life for me had been so different in the past four months that school seemed like it was for someone else.

What if Merlin knew someone there? What if someone — like an associate of Beto's - recognized me? I hadn't planned on that, hadn't thought that part through.

"When do I have to go?"

Bethany put her hand on her hips. "Tell you what. Since today's Thursday, how about we wait until tomorrow, and then you can have the whole weekend to get used to us. We're crazy, but at least we're normal crazy, and I think you'll fit right in. She walked over to Daniel and gave him a kiss on the cheek. "Gotta go now." She paused at the door. "Bye, Jesse — see you tonight, okay?"

"Oh-okay," I said, lifting a hand. She was gone.

I studied the guitars on the wall, unsure of what to do.

"You like my collection?" Daniel asked with a smile.

"Sure. They're cool." I reached out and touched the shiny red one that hung in the middle, slightly above the rest

"Do you play?"

"No." I picked one of its strings, the hollow tinny sound reverberating throughout the room.

"Here." Daniel stopped playing and pulled it gently off the wall. "This one's kind of special. Sort of an heirloom, I guess you could say. I've never even played it."

"You've never played it?" I frowned. "Why would you own a guitar that you'd never even play?"

He hesitated. "Sentimental reasons, I guess." He held it out. "Check it out—a vintage Gibson Les Paul. Mint condition, made custom back in 1956. See those dots? Real ivory inlay—they just don't make them like that, anymore."

"Ivory, like from elephants?"

"Uh-huh. Here—look at this finish—not a scratch on it." He turned it over and pointed to gold lettered numbers on the back. "It's even signed by the artist."

"Nice. Is it worth anything?"

"So they say." He cradled it in his arms and picked a string, adjusting the knobs a bit after. "I — I could teach you, you know. If you ever wanted to learn."

"No." I turned away from him. "I'm not going to be here that long, anyway."

"Well, you could be."

"Theo said I'm going into that group home pretty soon. You don't need to waste your time."

"I wouldn't be wasting my time, Jesse. I'd want to."

I saw the pity in his eyes and it made me cringe. Here I was, the poor orphan kid, the juvenile delinquent with the methed-out mom and stupid, shitty stepdad and a sister who was living god-knew-where.

"No, thanks," I said. I headed for the door. "You mind if I use your phone? I'm going to call Theo, find out what's going on."

The brightness in his eyes faded, and he placed the guitar carefully back on the wall. "Sure, go right ahead."

I felt bad for hurting his feelings, but I wasn't going to make the same mistake twice — get comfortable with people only to have them ripped away from me. It had happened too many times: Tim, Aurora, Indian. *Pony.*

I had to be smarter, this time.

Twenty-Eight

visit (v): to go to see.

I started school the following Monday, just as they said I would. It wasn't so bad, after all, and I hated to admit it, but I missed it—missed learning, missed doing something with my mind other than worrying about Merlin, Beto. Pony. The kids left me alone the way they do with new kids, and that suited me just fine. I didn't feel like one of them, anyway — with all their talk about college, grades, hookups, and weekend parties. I felt like a stranger, visiting a foreign country, with nobody speaking my language.

The nightmares still happened, but I never had another outburst like I did the first night. I tried to stay up as late as I could, watching TV, until a lot of times I woke up in the middle of the night on the couch.

It took a week of hassling Theo before he finally got me that visit with Pony, and it was set for an early Saturday morning. I went outside to wait for Theo and found Daniel sitting on the front steps, playing his acoustic guitar.

He looked up and grinned. "You excited for your visit?"

"I guess."

"You guess?" He shook his head, smiling.

"What? What's so funny?"

"Jesse, the mystery man. I've been watching you, and I think there's a lot more going inside of that head of yours than you let on."

I shrugged. "Think what you want."

He held my gaze for a minute, and then began playing. It was a sad melody, slow and sweet. When he was done, the last chord hung in the air until the notes just melted away. A few chickens scrabbled close to our feet.

"That song—what's it called?"

"Ah—so the stoic Jesse does have a heart. Redemption Song. Bob Marley, of course. One of the greats. The King of Reggae."

"What's it about?"

He stopped the strings with his palm, and rubbed his chin. "A bunch of things, in a way. He sings about slavery, both the real kind and the kind in your head."

Now the dreadlocks made sense. "I thought that guy just smoked a lot of pot," I said. "That's what this guy Merlin always told me."

He laughed. "Yeah, I think he did. I guess he had his own kind of mental slavery to deal with."

When he said that, I noticed a leather bracelet around his wrist with a little medallion that said *One Day at a Time*. I recognized that bracelet — lots of kids at the Hall wore them after their stints in rehab. I remembered what Bethany had said before, and I wondered why he went to AA.

Right then, Theo pulled up and honked the horn.

"Bye Jesse." Daniel rested his elbows on his guitar. "Have a nice visit."

*   *   *

"Here we are." Theo killed the engine and climbed out.

I had to wait two weeks until Theo finally set up a visit with Pony. It was at a park, because Theo said that the weather was nice and he thought it was best if we kept it on *neutral ground*, whatever that meant.

I stared out the window.

"Aren't you coming?" he asked, huffing. He wiped his brow.

It was the same park.

I couldn't move.

I recognized the line of cottonwoods, the cluster of picnic benches where the girl with chocolate hair fed the homeless people. Across the way, I spotted Beto's apartment complex.

Don't panic.

"Uh." I poked my head out of the cracked door. It was early on a Saturday morning and the park was empty, except for an Asian gang-banger walking his pit bull. But still, you never knew. "I dunno. Maybe we should do this another day."

Theo threw back his head and laughed, a great booming sound. "Are you kidding? Jesse, you've been on me for weeks about this visit. Come on. You finally get to see you sister."

"Fine."

I slouched out of the car and ducked my head forward, letting my overgrown bangs fall into my face. *You're being paranoid*, I told myself. *There's no way that Beto would be up this early, for one.*

I stole a quick glance over to the complex. Quiet.

Theo grinned. "Come on. Look, there they are. They just pulled up."

A brand new pearl-white Escalade parked on the other side, the side next to the swing sets.

My palms were faucets.

I didn't know why I felt so nervous. It was silly. She was my baby sister for crying out loud. Just a snot nosed brat who made my life crazy before this whole mess.

I stuffed my hands in my pockets and walked toward the swings.

A man and woman got out first. The woman had long, blond hair and was dressed like one of those mannequins at the mall. The man had a full head of hair and wore running shorts with a Nike ball cap. I saw his gold watch glint in the sun and even at a distance, I knew I hated him. Hated the both of them.

Frickin' Ken and Barbie.

The man opened the back door, and Pony stepped out.

Oh my God, she looked so different. Big, maybe a head taller than before. Her hair, it was short, cut to a bob just above her chin and she wore overalls with a pink turtleneck. She scanned the length of the park until she spotted me. Our eyes met.

"Jesse!" She ran toward me.

I left Theo behind, jogging ahead to cross the distance. My feet crunched across the dead fall leaves, and the sun shone thinly on my shoulders.

I held out my arms and she jumped into them. Just like in the movies.

"Pony." I buried my face in her neck. "I missed you," I whispered. She smelled like baby powder and maple syrup.

She giggled. "You have whiskers, now. You're tickling me." She squirmed away.

I smiled as I touched her cheek, rosy from the sun. "You look so big. And you're hair's different."

She patted her bob. "Mama Karen said that it's easier to comb this way."

"Mama Karen?" I looked up at the thin blond women standing nervously over by the trees.

"Her." She pointed. "My other mama."

The woman smiled weakly at me, and a course of anger rushed through my limbs. "You don't have another mama," I said, turning back to her. "Just one. Don't you remember Mom?"

"Theo?" The woman named Karen touched her neck, the glimmer of her diamond ring reflecting the sunlight.

"Yeah, uh, Jesse." Theo lumbered over and pushed a heavy hand on my shoulder. "Just keep it fun today, okay? Let's not talk about the past. You guys haven't seen each other in a long time and it's best to take advantage of your—"

"Come on, Jesse." Pony tugged on my arm. Let's play in the sandbox." I let her lead me away, but not before I gave the woman a glare. "I'm in kindergarten now. I have a backpack, and dolls, and my own room." She crouched down and began making a mound with the damp sand. I knelt beside her and helped make the mound bigger.

"Your own room? Wow."

I couldn't stop staring at her as she made her little sandcastle.

Her cheeks were fuller, rosier, and her hair shone, glossy and thick.

"Hey." I pulled up my sleeve and showed her my arm. "See this?" I asked, pointing to my tattoo.

"P-O-N-Y," she read slowly. "Po-nee. Pony?" She touched the blue lettering with her finger. "You wrote my name on your arm? That's silly," she said, laughing up at me.

"Yup." I felt a lump form in my throat. "So I wouldn't forget about you. You didn't forget about me — did you?" I pushed out a light laugh.

She stood up and brushed off the sand. "Mama Karen doesn't like to call me Pony," she said as she skipped toward the swing. With each step her sneakers lit up. "She says my birth name is Crystal but maybe we'll change it to Christine."

My heart, a ship against rocks.

"What did you just say?"

"Crystal?" called a female voice. She stood a few feet behind us and held out a puffy white jacket. "It's getting a little crisp. Would you like your coat?"

"It's still warm enough." I set my jaw and walked back over to the swings. "She's fine."

Pony sat on one and kicked her legs. "Jesse! Come and push me."

I pulled her back on the rubber swing and let her go, her body flying into the blue October sky.

"Ten more minutes," called Theo. The sound of his voice made my muscles tighten.

She flew back toward me, and I gave her another push. Nothing was going the way I thought it would.

"Jesse?" Theo tapped on his watch.

"All right, I heard you!"

Pony snapped her head around, her large brown eyes wide. I realized I was shouting. Theo and the Karen lady exchanged a glance.

"Fine," I said, a little softer.

I shot Pony a reassuring smile. I tried to focus on her, rushing through the air, her cheeks glowing in the wind.

It'll be okay, I thought. *She's the same. I'm the same.*

Only nothing was, anymore.

Twenty-Nine

permanent (n): 1. continuing or enduring;
2. without further change.

Theo pulled up alongside of the De Leon's house. "We'll do this again next week," he said with a self-satisfied smile. "How does that sound?"

I hated meeting Pony at a park like some stranger with her rich, snooty foster parents watching me as if I might jump her at any moment.

"I don't like those people. Why did they cut her hair so short? And why are they calling her Crystal?" I felt my lips curl as I thought about it. "Changing her name to Christine? You better put a stop to that crap, Theo."

He shifted the gear into park and paused, as if he was going to tell me something. "Tell you what. We'll know more at the court hearing next month. But you have to understand. Your mom's not going to get out for a few years. You kids need a permanency plan."

"Why can't we just get placed together? Like with the De Leons? I bet they'd take her in."

"No, Jesse." He sighed. "You don't understand. She's been with them a long time now…there's a bond. She's doing really well—can't you see that?"

I felt queasy. "What exactly are you saying? Just spit it out."

"You need to prepare yourself, Jesse."

"Prepare myself for what? What aren't you telling me?"

"You need to start thinking about your future." He hesitated before looking at me. "I wish you would talk to your mom. She wants the best for you."

I laughed, the bitter taste of it coating my mouth. "The best for me? That's rich."

"I'm taking Crystal to see her in jail. For a visit." He paused, studying me. "I think you should come, too."

"You're taking a little kid to visit a felon in jail? That's frickin' messed up, Theo."

"It's court-ordered. You're supposed to go, too, but apparently I can't make you."

"And Pony's too young to get to say no? That's twisted."

"She wants to see her birth mother, Jesse." He said it softly.

There was something strange in his voice. I looked at him hard, trying to figure out what he wasn't telling me.

"Well, I'm not going. Tell my mother she can kiss my ass. She's the one who got us in this mess in the first place."

He sighed, and for the first time I noticed the coffee stain on his buttoned-down shirt, the bags under his eyes. It made me wonder how long he'd been doing this dead-end job, playing babysitter to the children of low-lifes and bottom feeders.

"I know this is hard for you."

I leaned forward and pointed in his face. "You better fix this, Theo. It's not right, and you know it."

*   *   *

I walked through the front door and headed for my room, slamming the door behind me. I heard Daniel playing guitar in the room next to mine, but I didn't care if he heard.

I looked around the room, feeling tense, caged. I needed to do something, anything. I ripped the train covers off of the bed and threw them into a ball on the floor. I hated this room. Hated this foster home, hated Theo — hated everything.

A cast-iron train sat on the shelf and I grabbed it, feeling its weight in my hand, and in one quick motion, threw it against the wall. There. The plaster dented in, and the sight of the small hole in the wall made me feel better. I picked it up and threw it again, and again.

Prepare myself for what? What the hell did Theo mean? There was something wrong with the system when I couldn't even live with my own sister.

"Whoa!" I was about to let loose with another throw when Daniel busted in. "What the hell's going on?" He took in the hole, the train in my hand. "You put a damn hole in my wall, Jesse!"

I tried to throw it again when he grabbed my arm. "Cut it out —calm down!"

I was breathing heavily. "Or else…what? What are you going to do, kick me out? Good, because I don't want to be here anymore."

I struggled against his grip, firm around my upper arm.

"You're angry. Did something happen at your visit?"

I remembered the image of her jumping into that shiny white car, with her perfect shoes and new haircut — I lost her, I lost her when I had just found her.

"God, quit trying to help me." I wrenched my arm from his grasp. "You don't know who I am."

"Then tell me, Jesse! *Tell me.*" His eyes held mine.

My breathing came rapid and shallow and I could feel the adrenaline pumping as I let the words tumble out. "…You want me to open up? I'll tell you the whole fucking sob story of my life — will that make you feel better? 'Cause when I'm done, I don't think so."

"—Jesse—"

"I left her, okay?" My eyes watered as I remembered that night. "Hid her under a pile of moldy blankets and climbed out the back of the trailer like some river rat when the cops came knocking. I knew they'd get her, but I didn't care. Didn't care! I didn't give a shit and you know why?" I laughed, hard and bitter. "Because I didn't want to go back into foster care. Can you believe that? How fucked up is that for karma?"

He stood there with his hands on his hips, quietly taking it all in. "You think you're the only one who's made mistakes?" he asked in a low, steady voice. "Huh? Do you? I've made them, too."

"Oh, yeah?" I wiped away the snot that dripped from my nose. I was full-on crying now and I couldn't help it. "You kill anyone, Daniel? 'Cause I did — I killed my friend, the only friend I ever really had. I made him feel like such shit one day that he took a bag of H and snorted it until his heart stopped." I felt sick at the memory of Tim Em's eyes, half open and glassed over. "You really want me living with you? I don't think so. Let me go, and we'll all be happier."

I walked away from him in quick, angry strides. Group home my ass—I was sick of other people running my life. It was time to take charge again, and make some decisions on my own. I'd go to Arizona—to find Walter.

"I'm sorry about your friend," Daniel called out. "…I have that burden, too." He paused. "I killed my brother."

My feet froze.

"That's right." He stood still, his voice low. "He was seventeen when he died."

Was he lying? I couldn't tell. I turned around to face him. "What do you mean —you killed him?"

"There's a road about five miles from here that leads to a bunch of almond orchards. Back in the day, kids used to party deep in the trees, away from any cops or parents." He sighed. "We were driving home, and it was way past curfew. I was drunk. Should have never been driving. But I did, and misjudged the curve in the road. I wrapped our pickup around a tree. I was knocked clean out, and when I came to, he was… gone."

"I'm sorry. But it's not the same."

"Oh, no? You don't think I don't know how it is to live with guilt? I live with it every day. For a long time, I almost killed myself with trying to numb it. Jesse—" He took a step closer, and put his other hand on my shoulder, "My brother's dead. Your friend is dead. But Pony's alive — that ought to count for something."

His gaze was intense, and I looked away, thinking about the things I would have done differently in my life. Like taking Pony with me when I escaped. Not losing Beto's drugs. Being there for Aurora, so she didn't have to leave. Waking up before Tim was able to go to the bathroom.

Daniel's tone softened. "I spent a lot of years being messed up, until I met Bethany. Then I realized, you can never go back, only forward."

"What does even that mean, going forward?"

"Live your life. Graduate from school. Face your problems—if it were me, I'd go visit your mom, Jesse. If it were me, I'd have some questions for her. I think it's time."

Thirty

time (n): the measure of days.

We patched up the wall. And the more I thought about it, the more I realized that Daniel was right. It was time to patch a few other things up. It was time to talk to my mom.

*   *   *

I stood in the search line with Theo. Everyone else in the visitation building just waited patiently, as if they knew the routine.

"It's crowded today." Theo scanned the room.

Another social worker walked by with three little kids all dressed in their best clothes. Her badge read Hong Nguyen. "Hi Theo," she called, as the baby with a runny nose squirmed in her arms. "This is the second time this month I've seen you here. Long drive for you. Annette Garreth's kids?"

"Yup." He smiled his stupid puppy dog smile and jerked a thumb in my direction. "This is Jesse, the oldest. He's a good kid. It's his first time, today."

"Oh, how nice."

A loud wail erupted behind her. "He bit me!" The little girl, about three years old, yanked on the social worker's pants and began howling. The two-year-old boy, mugging a guilty look, took a step back.

"Oh, Marilyn, come here—" She bent down and hugged the little girl. The baby leaned forward and grabbed the girl's hair, causing her bawl to grow louder. "Here, let's go to the restroom," she said to the little girl, a flustered look on her face. "I think she's bleeding." She waved apologetically and made her way to the other end of the crowded room with all three kids crying.

I turned to Theo. "Don't do that again."

"Do what?"

"Talk about me as if I'm not here. I'm not a moron."

"Sorry, Jesse." He sighed and looked at the clock on the wall.

When it was our turn, we walked through the metal detector and were led to the search area. Two prison guards patted me down and had me pull out my pockets.

"This way," the taller one with a mustache said to the group. "Remember the rules; anyone that doesn't comply will have their visit terminated immediately. Everyone gets an hour."

We were led into the visitation room, which really looked like a school cafeteria, with glaring fluorescent lights and plastic tables and chairs. As the inmates filed in, their family members ran forward, hugging them and smiling.

Theo flapped his folder against his leg. "Nervous?"

"No."

I shook my hair out of my eyes and shoved my fingers in my back pocket. I hadn't seen her since June, six months ago. For so long, the anger I felt kept me going, warmed me up when I felt cold, and I didn't want to let it go.

And still, I wanted to see her. Crazy.

An inmate with long light-brown hair walked toward us with a timid smile on her face. I smiled politely at her.

"Jesse, can't you give your own mom a hug?"

I hardly recognized her. She had put on about twenty, thirty pounds, and her cheeks, once sunken in, were filled out. A pink bow, like the ones the girls in the Hall would wear on the side of their head, was stuck in her hair.

"...*Mom?*"

"Jesse." She hugged me and when she pulled back, her eyes were filled with tears. "I prayed to the Lord that you would come."

"I didn't know you guys were so tight."

"Come on, Jess." Theo gave me a watery smile and held out a chair for my mom. "Let's start this out on the right foot."

The three of us sat down at the table.

"I've changed, Jesse." She took a lock of her hair and wound it between her fingers, again and again. "Being in here has changed me, given me a new lease on life."

I looked at her coolly. "You sober?"

"Of course I am. Over 150 days of sobriety. One day at a time."

"Isn't it easy to get sober when you're locked up? I thought that was like, the general idea."

Theo shook his head and closed his eyes. I didn't care.

Mom's eyes flashed.

"You always did think you were better than me. It was the school that did it to you. That art teacher, putting all kinds of nonsense into your head, telling you that you could be something great."

I bristled at the mention of Mrs. Hamel, who always had my back. "She was the only one who cared if I went to school."

"You don't know what it was like," she said to Theo, "trying to raise two kids on my own. Darryl was never much help. It's hard work being a parent."

"I was the one who always took care of Pony," I said evenly. "And you know it. When you and Darryl were out getting wasted. Maybe you can explain that one to the Lord."

Her voice dropped into a hiss. "Don't you talk about my little baby. Don't you dare."

We glared at each other, and I felt like four months just melted away. What a family reunion — within two minutes, things were right back to normal.

"Annette?" Theo said weakly. "Maybe you should tell him now."

I stared at Theo, searching for clues. "Tell me what?" I asked.

Mom's eyes started to water. "No, Theo — you tell him. It doesn't matter anymore. Go ahead."

"Tell me what?" Underneath the table, I clenched my hands together. "Theo? Mom — what?"

"Oh, Jesse." She covered her face with her hands and began weeping. I felt numb, removed from it all, but I had to know — had to find out what was wrong.

"Jesse." Theo shifted his large body uncomfortably in the plastic seat. "Your mom wants to tell you — the reason I wanted you to come today — you need to know…. Jesse, Pony's being adopted."

Pony's being adopted.

Being.

Adopted.

"What?" I whispered. "Mom, we can't let them — the courts — are you fighting? Did you call your lawyer? Who? Those damn people at the park? —Mom, talk to me!"

She looked up at me, her eyes red and swollen. "I'm giving her to them, Jesse. I signed relinquishment papers. Last week."

"To those people?" I slammed my palm on the table. "No! They're not right for her, Mom! They're not her family — they don't care about her that way we do. You have to do something!"

"Jess—" Theo put a hand on my back and I shook it away.

"I'm doing hard time — going to be in here for four more years. Darryl for longer. And you know Darla can't do it — we have no other family, we have no other choice."

"I'm her family." I tried to keep my voice from cracking.

"Those people can do all kinds of things for her." Tears dripped down her face. "You think it's an easy decision for me? But it's Crystal's chance to get away from all this. Have the life she deserves to live. I don't want... I don't want another kid of mine..." She let her eyes drop.

"Another kid of mine... *what?*" My eyes flamed. "What the hell is that supposed to mean, Mom?"

"Look, I know, Jesse. I heard about juvie, running away, stealing the car..."

"I ran away because the cops were arresting you!" I stood up, and the chair clattered down behind me.

"—and Darla told me that you came to her house, and stole money from her boyfriend's wallet."

"Her—her boyfriend's a pervert! Did she tell you that? He

likes little girls, and guess what, Mom? Darla's a tweaker now, just like you."

Her eyes turned flat and cold. "Darla told me. You used the money for drugs."

"I have never done drugs!" I could feel my hands shaking as I backed away from the table. "I'm not like you."

A stab of pain seared across her face.

A prison guard stepped forward. "Is there a problem here?" He looked at the three of us with his hand on his service gun.

Theo scanned our faces. "Come on, guys," he said quietly. "Let's keep it together. This is supposed to be a nice visit. Come on, now."

I felt heaviness in my eyelids and closed them briefly. "What about me?" I said in a low voice. "What about my life?"

She sighed. "You'll do fine. You always were independent, even as a child. Thought it was weird at the time. You didn't need people like the rest of us. Like Crystal does."

Suddenly I wanted to be back home, down by the river's edge, at that time of day when everything was quiet, tinged with the orange of the fading sun. It was always the best time to swim, and I wanted to once again feel the weight of its currents pulling around me, taking me somewhere else, somewhere that wasn't my life.

"I took good care of her," I whispered. "When you weren't there. Which was always."

"That's it. I don't need to listen to this crap from my own son," she said, wiping her eyes. "I want this visit over. Guard?" She motioned for the guard against the wall to come closer. "I want to go back to my cell. Jesse — you can go to hell."

She stood up, gave me one last hard look, and allowed him to escort her toward the exit. And as I watched her leave, a dozen images flashed through my mind: of myself as a little kid, maybe no more than three or four, playing with sticks and rocks down by the river for half of the day, with no one to call me home; or when I was ten, listening to Pony as a newborn, scream for hours and hours, before I finally ran to the minimart to steal her some formula; every night I spent lying in bed, wondering if she would come home, hoping she was okay.

I was shaking.

"Hey, Mom." I called out. The room quieted a bit as people snapped their eyes toward me. She turned around and stood there, still tiny in her orange jumpsuit. From a distance, she looked young, like she could be my older sister. "You know what? You were right about me." Our eyes met. "I *will* be fine."

I just wish I could believe it.

Thirty-One

done (adv): not wanting to do more.

It was dark by the time Theo got me back home. He put the car into park. "It'll be okay, Jesse," he said. "You'll see."

"You mean my life?" I gave a short laugh. "Yeah, for sure."

"Hey." He pulled out a brochure from the yellow file and handed it to me. "I had some good news for you, but I wanted to wait. Here—check it out."

Golden Valley Home for Boys, it read. It was glossy and in full color, with pictures of clean-scrubbed boys wearing ridiculous-looking cowboy hats and sitting on a fence. The counselors looked happy and smiling, and the house was one of those white farmhouses you see in all the movies.

"This is your good news?" I handed him back the brochure.

"Jess, take a look — this place is only two hours from here," he said. "Up in the foothills. I think you'll really like it. They do all sorts of cool stuff: college prep courses, they help you get an apartment when you age out…And they'll transport you to visits with your sister. The Calloways are committed to letting you visit her, I want you to know that."

Letting you visit her.

"And that's it," I asked quietly. "I have to go?"

"I thought you hated living with the De Leons." He chuckled uneasily. "You told me once that their place is a dump."

"They're not so bad."

"Well, it was always temporary — you knew that, and so did they. Besides, they can't adopt until you leave, and they've been waiting a long time for a child."

I watched their house. The lights were on in the kitchen and I could see Bethany at the kitchen window, probably making dinner.

I was getting in their way. They were way too young, anyway — Bethany was only a couple years older than me, and Daniel only a few more. I thought of the little crib in my room, the trains on the bedspread. They were meant for someone else, for a different kid altogether.

"And they know?" I swallowed, my throat felt dry and needed water. "They know about the group home?"

"Yes. I told them today."

"Okay," I said, closing my eyes. "Okay."

*   *   *

I waited until I knew Daniel and Bethany were asleep.

My body was alert, buzzing with anticipation. I flung off the covers, fully dressed underneath. In the cover of darkness, I grabbed the trash bag of extra clothes from underneath my bed, and tiptoed out of the house, through the back door.

I was leaving.

They had known that something was up at dinner, but I chalked it up to my visit with my mom, said I was tired and just wanted to go to bed.

I walked silently through the backyard, past the chicken roosting in their old henhouse and the mulberry tree, surrounded by the waist-high weeds. I had all night in front of me, and I wanted to get some distance before they noticed that I was gone.

It made more sense this way, not saying goodbye. After all of it, Daniel and Bethany weren't so bad, and I didn't want them feeling guilty for wanting to adopt a little kid. They'd get over me. And Pony — I guess there was nothing else I could do, now. She had been swallowed up by another family, another life, and she didn't need me anymore.

The thought sunk to the bottom of my chest like a rock.

She didn't need me.

Well, I was done. Done letting other people control me, and I sure as hell wasn't going to end up in a group home, especially one that was hours away. I was going to Arizona. Walter said that the Havasupai were a small tribe, and everyone knew everybody else. Finding him should be easy enough. I could hitchhike there, and get a job. Be my own man, get away from this piss-small town and start over.

The forecast warned of rain, and the wind whipped in my face and my lungs burned with cold as I made it further down the street, further and further away. I ran straight for an hour, past the edge of town until I hit the highway.

The cars flew by me in both directions as I looked up at the sign. Which way was Arizona, I wondered? It was south, but did you have to go through Los Angeles to get there?

I headed south and stuck out my thumb. Maybe a trucker would know. Someone would have to know. The cold air flapped through my jacket and I cursed myself for not bringing a warmer one.

*　*　*

In the early morning, it started to rain. No one would give me a ride. And with every car that passed by, I held my breath, hoping it wasn't a cop looking for me.

I walked about five, maybe more miles before I came upon a truck stop. A long line of semis snaked through the wet darkness, and I stopped to watch a handful of truckers leave their cabs to head for the café, glowing yellow and crowded with dinnertime customers. Maybe someone here would give me a lift, or at least give me directions. At least it would be good to get out of the rain for a little bit.

I started walking through the slickened parking lot, when a girl came up to me out of nowhere, a gas can in her hand. Her face was smeared with heavy makeup and she wore a Raiders T-shirt, see-through from the rain, and cut so that it barely covered her chest. She was young, too—maybe just a few years older than me, I guessed.

"You got any extra cash?" she asked, with squeaky, surprisingly high-pitched voice. "My car ran out of gas."

Where had she come from?

I glanced around. "Where's your car?"

She smiled at me and smoothed her wet hair behind an ear, all at once slow and seductive. "Or maybe you just need a good time."

"Huh?" I bent closer, thinking I misheard her.

She sidled up closer to me, her breath smelling sickly sweet. "A good-looking boy like you, ain't you never had a good time?"

"Uh…" I was speechless for a moment, stunned, until I saw the track marks on both of her arms. "…A good time? I thought you said that your car—"

"Look, dude." She jiggled the gas can, and tilted her head with an irritated, impatient expression. "You gonna help me out or not, cause it's frickin' cold out here, and I don't got all night."

"I'm-I'm sorry…I don't have any money." I only had the five dollars that Bethany and Daniel gave me every day for lunch money, and that was going to pay for my breakfast. I couldn't give her that, not when it was all I had. I looked at her face—her cheeks were still full, but she had that junkie's twitchy, jerky way of moving. "What's your name?" I asked, stalling.

"Destiny. What's yours?"

"Jesse."

"Jesse, I like that name. So, come on." She pressed up closer to me, steering us closer to the line of bushes behind the parking lot. "Just a couple of bucks, I know you got a couple of bucks." She began pulling at my jeans, undoing the belt that held them up. The rain hit the leaves on the bushes behind us in a soft, pattering rhythm as I watched her fingers, thin and white, as they opened up my belt, tugged at the zipper—

I began to feel sick. "No," I said, pulling her up, "No—hey, let's just go inside and we can get something to—"

"See," she leaned her face in closer, inches away from my lips, "you do have money, I knew you did. Come on, I'll make it worth your while—"

"No!" I pushed her off, and tried to steady myself, tried to stop my stomach from heaving. "Just stop."

"Asshole!"

She flounced away in an angry huff and I stood there and watched as she approached one, then another trucker, making her way down the line until finally, one—an ancient-looking guy with a foot-long beard, put his arm around her and opened the door to his cab. It was a long silver truck, and the side read: *Galvin and Sons Trucking Co., Little Rock, Arkansas.*

Something snapped inside me when I saw that door close.

I thought of Walter, that hardened look on his face, that glazed over expression he had before he headed into those apartments, like his soul went someplace else.

It wasn't right—she was so young, about my age—

"Hey!" I ran toward the truck, the fresh rain puddles splashing beneath me. "Hey, wait!" I jumped up on the foot landing of the semi and started banging on the passenger door. "Open up! I'll give you the money—I'll give you the money—"

The door opened, and I jumped off onto the asphalt. The guy in the beard peered out and glared down at me. "What in the hell do you think you're doing?"

The rain dripped down my face but I could see the girl through the crack in the door. "Tell her I found some money, tell her I want to talk to her."

He looked me up and down and spat onto the ground. "Get

the fuck outta here, kid."

"Hey!" I looked around, panicked. "Help! There's a girl in here, with this guy—"

He jumped out of the cab and yanked me by the throat, banging me into the side of his truck. "I *said*, get the fuck outta here, if you know what's good for you. Mind your own business."

He released his hold on me and I gasped, sucking in breath. I staggered back and spun around, looking blindly in all directions. The parking lot was empty, and I heard the whirl of the highway in front of me. The door to the cab slammed, and I saw the light of dawn glimmer in the distance through the rain.

I started running toward the highway.

She was so young — I should have given her the money. The trucker's face, with his long beard, and his worn, craggy face flashed before me. She was so young.

All at once, I felt my breath quicken, the way it had dozens of times before, my heart racing forward, as if trying to escape something, a memory deep within me that had been trying to bubble forward this whole time.

And then the world caved in.

I squeezed my eyes shut. The ugliest memory, the one that I hid deep inside me somewhere, rose to the surface.

He smelled like black licorice.

My foster parents were older, so I called them Grandpa Gus and Grandma Jean. She had the softest lap and made the best oatmeal raisin cookies I had ever tasted and I never wanted to leave until Grandpa Gus started making his visits to me in the middle of the night, for what he called our special time.

I never told anyone.

I was eight, and my room had trains.

*   *   *

The rain slowed to a sprinkle, and the cars continued to fly past me as I ran. A part of me knew that I should get off the highway, hide myself — that it would be too easy for the cops to spot me, but I didn't care. It was like a different part of me was watching my own self from somewhere else, somewhere far above, and away.

Tears stung my eyes, and I wanted to escape, wanted it all to go away, but I couldn't. No matter how hard I ran, I couldn't run away from what was in my head.

I saw a flash of blue light and heard the crunch of gravel in front of me. A car had pulled over onto the side and the driver flung open the door and jumped out, running toward me.

Thirty-Two

```
found (v): recovered.
```

Jesse! Thank God, I found you." Daniel ran up and grabbed my arm. "I can't believe it — we've been searching for hours." His face was strained and bleary with sleep.

I wanted to hug him, I was so glad to see his face, but instead I turned away, wiping my eyes. "Just go home, Daniel."

"Go home?" He laughed flatly. "Are you kidding? No way — I just found you, Jess. Come and get in the car."

I dug my fists deep in my pockets. "I can't."

"Why can't you? Jesse — why did you run? Is this about your mom? When we found you missing, I called Theo, and he said that you were pretty upset. I wish we had known — he didn't tell us. I wish we could have talked about it."

"It doesn't matter. I'm done. Call the police if you want, but I'm not going back." I began walking toward Los Angeles. The cars blared past as I walked over the gravel, broken beer bottles and dirty diapers cluttering the way.

He kept pace with me. "Where are you headed?"

"Does it matter?"

"Well, yeah! It does to me. To Bethany."

I shook my head. "Look, I've already decided. I've got plans, and I'm not letting them put me in some group home."

"No." He shook his head. "Me neither."

I stopped walking. "You're trying to adopt. Theo said that you're on hold until I'm gone."

"Bethany and I — we've talked." He gave a small smile. "Look. We want you to stay. If you want, that is."

"No! I don't want your pity."

"What makes you think it's pity? God, Jesse, quit being so stubborn!" He took an angry breath.

I hesitated. "But Theo—"

"We've already talked to Theo. He said that he'd put off the group home, if you agree — if we found you. It's your choice."

I thought of the room I slept in, with the trains and the teddy bear. "They won't give you a baby, not when you have me living with you."

"We're young, Jesse." His brown eyes were kind. "That can wait."

"I don't know." I felt the tears, hot and stinging behind my eyes. "I don't know."

He reached for me, and pulled me into a hug. "Listen." His voice was low, patient. "You don't have to make a decision right now. There are no prison bars in our house. Just come home with me, and think about it. See how things go."

I took a deep, ragged breath, and for the first time, that shadow that had always been present in my life, hovering like a ghost on the edges of my mind, seemed to go away a little bit, fade from the deepest black to gray.

I closed my eyes. "Okay. We'll see how things go."

*   *   *

Life started to change.

I couldn't explain it, but after that night, something inside me broke — something hard and brittle, like ice from the mountains thawing out from a long winter.

For the first time in a long while, I felt like I was thawing out.

I was able to see Pony every week. It was still hard, seeing her so happy with her foster parents, but after a while I started to accept it.

She was happy, I reminded myself.

That should count for something.

Going to school got easier, and pretty soon I got to know a few of the kids who lived around us.

I had promised myself that I would never draw again, but that was one promise I couldn't keep. Not with Bethany around. Once she found out that I could draw, she set me up with my own art set — brand-new sketch pads and pencils, the nice ones, like the kind you could only buy at an art store.

When I got home from school, I would go outside and find a quiet place to draw, out by the chicken coop, or next to the overgrown vegetable garden. Within a week, I had filled up an entire pad with drawings.

"Jesse, this is really good," Bethany said in a quiet voice as she flipped through the pages. She paused on one of Walter. I drew him up on a horse, with his hair long and caught up in the wind. "You have a gift."

"Thanks." I felt my face flush and took the sketchpad back. It's what the girl at the park had said, so many months ago. It wasn't easy accepting a compliment — I never looked at my artwork as a gift, just something I did, a part of myself.

For my sixteenth birthday, Daniel decided that he should teach me how to play guitar.

For some reason, I let him.

We sat in their cramped little art room most evenings, once I finished my homework. Already I could play most chords, if I went real slow. I tried to keep it from Daniel, but I was kind of proud of myself.

Daniel pulled off the shiny red one from its place on the wall. "Tonight I'm going to teach you another classic. *No Woman, No Pride.* There are just four chords, so once you learn them, you can play the whole song."

I stared at the Gibson, shiny and as gleaming as those red candy apples you got from the fair. "You're letting me play that one?"

He nodded with a grin and held it out to me. "Sure. Go ahead."

"But — but you never play that one. You never touch it. It's too special."

"Nah." He nudged me. "It's okay, Jesse. I want you to. It's time for someone to play it."

I held it in my hands, feeling its weight — it was heavy and cool against my palms.

He reached out and stroked the neck almost lovingly, but his eyes held something that I had seen there before, when he talked about somebody else.

I strummed a C chord and looked at him, suddenly realizing. "It was Nate's, wasn't it?"

"Yup." He smiled tightly. "Go ahead," he said, gesturing with his hand. "Play something."

I picked out an F chord. My fingers smarted from all the new calluses.

"So was he any good?"

He smiled, the memories flooding his face. "Are you kidding? That kid was a complete natural. He had a photographic memory. Perfect pitch too, the bastard. But of course, he was more into metal." He inclined his head in my direction. "Go on — are you going to play or not?"

"Pipe down," I said, enjoying teasing him. "I'll do my best."

Thirty-Three

precipice (n): on the edge.

The bus doors opened, and I stepped onto the dirt road. It was the last day of school before Christmas vacation, and the fog had burned off into a hazy mist. I hoisted my backpack over my left shoulder and began to walk the half a mile toward Daniel and Bethany's house.

"Jesse, wait up." Hailey, a girl from my European History class, jogged up to catch me. "How'd you do on the test? I think I choked. Boy, Williamson can sure be a hard-ass."

I shrugged. "I think I missed that whole section on the Jacobin regime."

"Me, too." She scoffed. "I'll be lucky if I get a C in that class. Hey, are you going to Steve Johnson's party Saturday?" she asked. "I hear it's supposed to be pretty sick."

"No."

She tilted her head. She was cute in a cheerful, freckly sort of way. "Don't you ever get to go out? Are your foster parents super strict or something?"

"They're not too bad."

She tossed her auburn ponytail. "One of these days, you'll have to come out with us. It'll be fun."

Maybe she liked me. But you never could tell for sure with girls.

I wasn't quite ready for girls. Every time I talked to one, I thought of Aurora. I thought of her almond-shaped eyes and the teardrop shaped tattoo that she got in memory of her dead brother. I wondered if she got another one for her baby. Thinking of her still hurt pretty bad.

"Maybe one of these days," I said finally.

A car passed with a Christmas tree strapped to the top. I pointed. "I think we're getting one of those tonight."

I played it off like it was no big deal, but secretly, I was kind of excited. Daniel and Bethany kept talking about this place up in the mountains where you cut your own trees. We were going there right when I got home. I never got to pick out a Christmas tree, ever, in my whole life. The years we did have one, Mom and Darryl got them like the day before Christmas, when they practically were giving them away.

She closed her eyes and inhaled. "I love Christmas. Don't you?"

I was just about to answer her when an orange car pulled up alongside of us. An orange El Camino, to be exact.

The window rolled down.

"Hey, Jesse." Merlin leaned over from the driver's side. His hair was still long, but his face had changed. It was yellowish, and thinner. The scar was still there, a jagged red line, and a cluster of sores spotted his cheeks. "We all miss you on the east side."

I stopped midstride. My heart pounded like a hammer inside my chest as I bent down to make eye contact.

"Hi, Merlin," I said evenly. I took in the meth sores. "You look like shit."

"And you look like someone who has a death sentence, bro." His yellowed eyes darkened. "I told you I'd find you. Just a matter of time. Apparently you're stupider than I thought. A smarter kid would have cleared out of this place months ago."

My heart sunk like a stone when I realized he was right. I was an idiot for thinking that they'd simply forget about me. But I showed my best poker face.

"So when did you go from smoking joints all day to becoming Beto's henchman?" I shook my head. "You like being in bed with the devil?"

"You're in bed, too, Jesse. And you know it."

The way he said that sent a chill up my spine. "Look," I said, glancing over at Hailey. She couldn't hear but she could tell something was up. She shifted her backpack to the other shoulder and swayed nervously. "Tell Beto I can get it. The money. Just give me some time."

His voice dropped an octave. "Time's up, pretty boy. And we've added a late payment penalty. Which makes the amount a grand total of $3,000. By Monday. Each day you're late, we tack on another grand."

The blood drained from my face. "There's no way, Merlin. There's absolutely no way—"

His eyes flashed. "She lives at 6425 Melody Lane," he said through gritted teeth. "Her foster parents are Mr. and Mrs. Calloway. She has short hair, now, and wears those cute little sneakers that light up when she walks." He picked up his phone and showed me a picture. It was a grainy shot of Pony taken through a chain-link fence. It looked like she was on a playground.

My hands shook. "You wouldn't," I whispered.

"She takes ballet on Wednesday, and she's in kindergarten at Greenway Elementary. Oh yes, Jesse. I would, and I *will*." He lifted up his shirt and reached into his waistband. There was a dull flash of gray as he held out a gun and pointed it at me.

"Jesse!" Hailey let her backpack drop and edged backward.

I stared at the barrel of the gun.

"Go home," I yelled to her. "You'll be fine." I tried to nod and motioned with my chin for her to keep walking. She stood still, frozen.

"Yeah, sweetheart," Merlin called, the gun still pointed at my face. "Go on home. Don't waste your time messin' with boys from Bravo Hills." He laughed as she began walking quickly down the road. "We're nothing but white-trash trouble."

I closed my eyes and swallowed, desperately trying to think. "I need longer than Monday."

"No. Don't push me, Jess." He clicked off the safety. "Pony sure won't look as cute with a bullet hole in her forehead."

The earth tilted on its axis.

"Stop, please. Just stop." I wet my lips. "Fine. Monday."

He smiled. "Do you still have my number?"

I nodded.

"That's better, Jesse. Let me know when you got it. We'll be in touch."

He peeled out, the dirt kicking up in my face.

*   *   *

Hailey was sobbing by the time I caught up with her.

"Please don't say anything to anybody," I said. I pulled on her arm until she stopped walking. She spun around and faced me. "Look, I'm begging you. It's for your own safety, and the De Leons. They're good people; they don't deserve to have any more trouble brought their way."

She stopped in front of her house, a long ranch identical to mine, only painted a faded avocado green. A horse standing in their pasture raised its head and whinnied.

"Who are you?" she said to me, her eyes flashing. "Like a drug dealer or something? And who was that strange-looking guy? He had a gun. Was that a real gun?"

I shook my head. "Hailey, please. I'll explain later. I think I can figure this out, but if you tell anyone, people could die."

But not just people.

Pony.

I could still see the picture of her in my head.

Hailey glanced toward her house. It was growing dark by now and her father stood on a ladder, hanging Christmas tree lights on the front gable.

"You owe me for this," she said, her voice shaking. "And if anything happens to you, it's not on me."

I exhaled a ragged breath. "Everything will be okay, I promise. You'll see, I can make this right."

I had to.

Thirty-Four

decision (n): a determination arrived after
consideration.

I walked through the front door, my forehead clammy with sweat. Bethany sat in the living room going through boxes of Christmas decorations. She wore a tie-dyed Grateful Dead sweatshirt with green stretch pants and black fuzzy boots.

"Oh, good, you're home. Look," she said, holding up a bundle of knotted Christmas lights. "Fiasco around here. Do you want to help me?"

"No." I shrugged off my backpack and headed toward my room.

"Aw, come on, Jesse." She smiled and tilted her head. "Pretty please?"

My head snapped in her direction. "I said, no, goddammit!"

Her eyes went wide. I went inside my room and slammed the door.

I slid down against the wall, covering my mouth with my

hands. My lungs strained for oxygen, and every breath I took seemed to not be enough.

What was I going to do?

How was I going to come up with that kind of money, and in that short amount of time?

Twenty minutes later, I heard a knock on my door.

"Jesse." It was Daniel's voice. He knocked again, and then walked in. His hands rested on his hips. "Please explain to me what's going on."

I glared up at him. "Nothing."

His mouth was set in a hard line. "I don't appreciate you talking to Bethany like that. No matter what happened to you today, she doesn't deserve it."

I laughed bitterly. "Fine. I'll tell her sorry. Is that better?"

"No, actually." He peered closer. "Jesse, did something happen at school? Did you blow that history test?"

"Daniel, please just leave me alone." I wiped my face with my hands.

"What if I don't want to leave you alone? What if I want to help you talk about it? Because it feels better when you talk about what's bugging you."

"I don't want to talk about it, okay?" I realized that I was shouting. "Because maybe, there's nothing to really talk about it. Maybe I'm just sick and tired of the perfect family routine and I just want you and Bethany to leave me the FUCK ALONE!"

We stared at each other.

"I don't believe you," he said finally, in a low voice. "Jesse, we've made a connection in these last few months, and I know that there's a lot inside that heart of yours. You've—"

"Let me spell it out for you, Daniel. I'm not your stupid brother, okay? He's dead, and I'm different. And you're not my dad or brother or whatever in the hell you think you are."

"Wow. Okay. That hurt." He sat down on my bed. "But I guess that's what you wanted to happen, right? Well you win, buddy. You got me. Point one for Jesse Sampson. Do you feel better now? 'Cause I'm guessing you still feel like shit on the inside."

"Fuck off."

He stood up. "Fine. Have it your way. But just so you know, we will be outside in the kitchen for approximately ten more minutes before we leave to go and cut down a Christmas tree. If you can come out and apologize to the both of us, we would love to have you join us."

"No, thanks. I'd rather stay right here." I could see the pain in his eyes, but I pressed forward. "And I've been thinking, that maybe I should go into that group home after all. Might be a good idea. I don't really like all the rules around here, and I really need to start thinking about myself."

He stood by the doorway and pressed his lips together. "Fine, Jesse. Do what you want."

"I'm going to call Theo, see if there's still space."

He swallowed. "That would be your decision, and you're certainly in a position to make it."

"It is."

He gave me one last look, and then quietly closed the door.

Ten minutes later, I heard the sound of their car drive away.

I hugged my knees to my chest and fell to the carpet. I never in my whole life hated myself so much. Daniel didn't react the way I wanted him to. I wanted him to shout back, yell, call me an asshole, kick me out, *anything*. Anything but what he did—treat me with decency.

I hated the way that Hailey looked at me, like I could have hurt her or something. *Who are you?* she asked me. That was the same thing Abuelo asked so many months ago up in the Grapevine.

I spotted the Swiss Army knife that Daniel had given me lying on the floor. I grabbed it and opened up a blade. It glittered in the dim light as I turned and twisted it in my hand.

Maybe it would be easier on everyone if I just ended it, right here, right now. I pressed the blade deep against my wrist. A thin bead of blood pooled up, a bright ruby drop against my flesh.

I bit my lip, sucking in my breath.

How hard would it be to die? How hard could it really be to just open up my veins, and allow all that was keeping me living to flow out? I dragged the blade up against my arm, the line of blood following behind the point. The pain that followed made me wince, but it felt good.

I watched the blood drip down my arm and onto the carpet. Now I understood why Tim liked to cut himself. The best way to fight pain is with pain you get to inflict yourself.

I grabbed a T-shirt from the floor and held it against the shallow wound. I couldn't do it. Not because I was a coward, but because if I died, Merlin could still come after Pony.

Three days. Three days to come up with more money than I'd ever seen in my whole life. Maybe I could rob a bank. Except, there was a good chance I'd get caught, and there's no telling I would be able to get the money to Merlin. I couldn't risk it. Robbing a store wouldn't work, either. It would be too hard to rob enough stuff to add up to $3000, and besides, then I'd have to sell it. I could deal drugs. But I didn't know anyone in the business on this side of town, and obviously I couldn't ask Merlin.

And then, it hit me over the head. It was so freakin' obvious. How did I not think of it sooner? The guitar. Nate's guitar. Daniel said it was valuable. I could hock it at a pawn shop. I padded down the hallway and opened the door to the music room. In the darkness, I could see Nate's guitar hanging with the others on the wall. Really, it was just too easy.

Who are you? Abuelo's voice seemed to whisper in my ear. I shook my head. Not now. I didn't need some type of guilt trip right now.

I'm Jesse, I wanted to shout. *I'm not this. I'm not a thief, not a drug dealer.* What did Abuelo say anyway, right before they dropped me off in Long Beach? Something about having to go through the bad to get to the good.

So I'd steal the guitar. And then, I'd have to leave, vanish forever, far away from Merlin and Beto and the De Leons and all the shit that would be left in my wake.

But Pony. I'd never see her again. I'd never know if she was ever, truly safe. No. I couldn't let that happen. Couldn't live with that. I *wouldn't* let that happen, not when I've come so close. Walter may be gone, but I made him a promise back in that orange grove.

To find Pony.

But more importantly, to get her back. And suddenly, it all became crystal clear. Walter said it first.

I'd kidnap her.

Thirty-Five

pawn (n): to sell an object in exchange for
money.

Everything had to be timed perfectly. Nothing could go wrong, or it would all collapse, like a house of cards.

I waited until Sunday night.

The De Leons were planning on serving meals to the homeless down at the Mission, the shelter off of E street. It sounded cool. I was looking forward to going, before my encounter with Merlin and before my future fell into a drastic tailspin away from any kind of normal life.

I had apologized to them over the weekend. It was a relief when they accepted. They didn't deserve how I acted, or what I was about to do.

Daniel and Bethany grabbed their coats and headed toward the door. I laid on the couch in the sunken living room, flipping through the channels.

"Jesse?" Bethany had her purse on her shoulder, the keys to their beater truck in her hand. "Aren't you coming, tonight?"

I felt my forehead and groaned a little. "I don't feel so good. I think I might have a fever."

She furrowed her brow, walked over to me, and stretched out her hand. It felt cool against my skin. "Hm. You do feel a little flushed."

"Yeah. I've been getting the shakes and stuff." And I held a hot washcloth against my skin, but she didn't know that.

She tut-tutted and left to go get me some Nyquil. I turned over on the couch and fluffed the brown pillow.

"Jess?" Daniel poked his head around the corner. "You're really going to miss it?"

"Sorry. I wanted to go, really. Next time, okay? I promise." I swallowed slowly.

They exchanged a quick glance, and then Daniel nodded. "Okay. Feel better, bud. I'll have my cell if you need me."

I waited about thirty minutes until I was sure they were gone. The music room was closed and I slowly creaked it open. Adrenaline pumped through my veins.

There hung Nate's guitar.

"Don't be a chicken," I whispered. I walked over and lifted it off the wall. It felt heavy in my hands. Would it be worth enough? I guess I would soon find out. I stared at it for a moment before putting it in its case. Any guilt I felt I stuffed down deep. There was no time for second thoughts.

I grabbed the keys to Bethany's car from the hook in the kitchen. I looked around the house. The Christmas tree we decorated yesterday glowed from its spot in near the front window. *God,*

I was a piece of shit.

On impulse, I pulled off a sheet of the shopping list. *Forgive me. Jesse,* I wrote. I went out the back door and into the foggy night.

*   *   *

There were only a couple of pawn shops open late on a Sunday night, and I chose the one in the worst part of town. I parked the car on the side of the road, grabbed the guitar, and walked inside.

The doorbell jingled. The store was jammed full of stereos, television, and instruments. The carpet was a stained mossy green.

The lady at the counter had a silver bouffant hairdo and a sweatshirt embroidered with sequined mistletoe and the words *Pucker Up.* A cigarette dangled out of her mouth. She glanced up at the clock. "We're closing at ten. You need to make it quick."

"Sure." I squeezed the case through the front. "I like your top."

She looked down and brushed away some lint. "Thanks," she said, smirking a little. "I made it myself."

"Really?" I sat at a chair next to the counter. "I like it."

She furrowed her brows, as if she didn't know quite what to make of me, and frowned. "Don't shovel me horseshit, son. What do you got?"

I pulled the case up onto the counter and opened the latches. "This. I'd like to sell it."

She put on her glassed and peered closer. She whistled. "A vintage Gibson Les Paul. Custom?"

I nodded.

She whistled again and lifted it out of the case. "Who'd you steal this from?"

"Steal it?" I shook my head and widened my eyes. "Oh, no ma'am, I certainly didn't steal this. You ever hear of The Roundabouts?"

She wrinkled her nose. "Maybe. They played local?"

"Yup. You hear of Darby McCallis?" I made up the name in an instant.

"No."

I lifted my eyebrows. "My grandpa. He gave me this guitar just before he died."

Her face remained slack. "Yeah? So why are you selling it?"

"Don't play. Plus, my mom really needs a car, and I wanted to surprise her with the money for Christmas."

She frowned again. "Instruments aren't my specialty. And the economy is still plumb rotten. Still, I'll see what we can manage. Earl?" She craned her neck toward an open back door. "Earl? Get on in here, we have a customer."

There was a dusty old cuckoo clock above the cash register and I watched the big hand on the face sweep its way toward the top.

"What? Do you want to close on time or not? I need to check inventory before tomorrow, Mabel." An old man half the size and weight of Mabel hobbled into the room. He had a hunched back and papery, translucent skin. "What is this?" he said, looking at the guitar.

"Kid says it's his grandpa's."

He sucked in his breath and picked up the guitar. "What is this, a '55, '56?"

I kept my expression neutral. Never show 'em how hungry you are. "Not sure. I think he said something about it being made in 1956. It was his favorite guitar."

Earl turned the instrument over in his hands, scrutinizing every angle. "Huh." His eyes glimmered a little bit. "Hold on, let me see what I can do." He shuffled away and disappeared again through the back door.

Mabel and I stood there and smiled awkwardly at each other in the silence. A static-y version of Silent Night played on the radio. The fog hovered outside of the window.

"Okay." Earl shuffled back in, carrying a dog-eared book in his hands. "This is what I can do for you. I'll take it for $1500 dollars."

I flushed. "Are you kidding me? Grandpa said it was worth more like twenty thousand."

He nodded, and licked his lips. "It's a nice guitar. But I got lots of nice guitars in the back. I'm giving you a deal by offering $1500. I should be only going a grand, but since it's Christmas and all, I figured I'd be generous."

It takes a con to smell a con. Was I a con? I didn't have a clue anymore. All I knew was this was my only chance.

But I could sense his eagerness. He wanted it.

"Nope." I closed the case, sweat prickling along the back of my neck. "No way. Grandpa would kill me if I let it go. My friend said I could sell this thing on eBay for at least five grand, so maybe that's what I'll do." I picked up the guitar, and headed toward the front door. "Thanks anyway."

My hand grasped the brass doorknob.

"Fine." He sighed dramatically. "Two grand. That's the best I can offer."

I turned slowly on my heel. "Four. I can't go lower. The car my mom needs is four. I know this guitar is worth a lot more."

He ducked his head, and smiled. "Ah, kid. I'm always a sucker for a good sob story. And you seem like a good kid. Okay. I can do three, and not a penny more."

I met his gaze. "Deal."

Thirty-Six

kidnap (n): to carry away by an unlawful force.

The folded money felt thick in my back pocket. I drove onto the freeway, heading toward Pony's house. Thank God I had lifted her address from Theo's precious yellow folder weeks back. I kept her address in my pocket, never sure why I did. Maybe some part of me always wanted to do this, take her away on my own terms. Like a vigilante from one of those movies. Maybe it took Merlin's threat to finally push me over the edge.

The clock read 10:38. I didn't know how much longer I had until the De Leons came home. Minutes, maybe.

I stepped on the gas. There was no time to lose.

I pulled up to the front gate of the Falcon Lake neighborhood. The water of the man-made lake and the fountain reflected through the windshield.

Damn. I hadn't planned on a gated community. How was I supposed to get in? Who even did that?

Rich people.

Snobby, stuck-up rich people. I was doing her a favor by taking her away from these people.

But still, I had to get in.

Two more minutes passed. This could all blow up in my face if I didn't play it cool.

Finally, a silver convertible pulled up behind me loaded with drunk high school girls. I did a quick inventory in the rear-view mirror to make sure I didn't know them. One glance told me they were from the south side, dressed in tight designer jeans and diamond studs in their ears. There was no way they'd ever rub elbows with a Bravo Hills boy.

The car honked.

I opened my door, and leaned out. "Ladies," I said, flashing my best, most charming smile. "I'm here for a party. Do you know the code?"

Within the car erupted a chorus of giggles. The driver, a cute brunette, met my gaze. "No, way! Are you going to Ryan's, on the lake?"

"Yeah. For sure. You?"

Another round of giggles. "You bet. Here, I'll buzz you in."

"Thanks." I smiled at her. "See you inside."

"Okay." The brunette smiled back and dipped her head coyly. She pulled her head in and drove up to the gate. It opened, and I followed close behind.

I passed by the house I guessed to be Ryan's. Cars flooded the driveway and red plastic cups littered the front lawn. I waved to the group of girls from the convertible as they made their way toward the front door. They watched me with confused expressions as I drove the opposite way.

It might be fun to go to a party some time, to be a normal teenager who wasn't worried about social workers and drug dealers and friends who OD'ed. But maybe, for all I knew, that was what real high school was like. It didn't matter anymore, because it was all too late.

The house was nestled at the end of a quiet cul-de-sac. Through the fogged windows, I could hear the thumping music of the party across the lake.

I parked in front of a darkened house and got out.

The air was cool on my skin. The Calloway house was a large two-story, covered with ivy. A Christmas tree glowed in the front window, and a herd of twinkling reindeer stood on the lawn. Their mechanical heads bobbed up and down in a jerky way, and they seemed to be staring at me, as if they were surprised to see me in front of their house.

A car drove down the main road and I dove into a bunch of bushes. I forced myself to breathe normal. If anyone stopped me, I'd play dumb, and pretend that I was looking for the party.

Except for the Christmas tree, the house looked dark.

What if someone was up?

It didn't matter. This was my last and only chance. For all I knew, Daniel and Bethany could be home already, and the cops could be already on their way.

I ran toward the front window on the right. I was pretty sure it was Pony's room. She always talked about how she liked to look out her window and watch the cars go by. The shutters were closed. I closed my eyes, took a deep breath, and rapped softly.

"Pony," I whispered. "Wake up."

I couldn't hear anything inside. Shit. She always was a deep sleeper. I'd have to open the window up. I pulled out the pocket-knife from my back pocket and pried open the screen. The windows were older, thank God, and would be a piece of cake to open. I dug my fingers into the edge of the glass and pulled.

The glass squeaked. My breathing hitched up ten notches.

Please, let this be your room.

I had the window opened by an inch. It was her room, all right—it was all pink. Pink, with a mural of ponies and her name painted in polka-dotted lettering on the far wall. Underneath a canopied bed, I could see her little body covered by a pink comforter. I slid the window open the rest of the way and heaved my body inside.

Her bedroom door was closed. That was good, it would buy me more time.

She shifted under her covers and mumbled something in her sleep.

"Pony." I jostled her shoulder. "Wake up, Pone. It's me, Jesse."

She jerked away, sucking in her breath sharply. "Jesse?" she said in a loud, high voice. "What are you—?"

I clamped my hand across her mouth. "Quiet," I whispered, my eye on the door. I could see the fear and confusion in her widened eyes. I forced myself to smile. "It's a surprise, Pone. I'm here to take you on a trip. A Christmas trip. You'll be quiet?"

She nodded.

I released my hand.

"Where are we going? Disneyland?" She hugged a rag doll I'd never seen before close to her chest.

"No. Not this time. Somewhere more special, though. I

promise." I picked her up and grabbed a blanket from her bed, wrapping it around her.

"I want my suitcase. I have a Hello Kitty one."

I grabbed a pair of her shoes lying on the floor and a jacket hanging off a hook. "No, honey. We'll have to come back for that. Okay?" I held her close to me and lifted a leg over the window-sill.

"I want to say goodbye to my Mommy Karen." Her voice lifted into a whine.

"No, no. That's part of the surprise. We'll call them and tell them goodbye, later."

Tears caught in her throat. "And then we'll come back?"

This wasn't going the way I thought it would. I hadn't figured on her not completely eager to come with me. Her arms were wrapped around me, but still, she seemed scared.

"…Jesse?"

I kissed her hair. "Then we'll come back."

"Okay, Jesse."

My eyes smarted. I couldn't stoop any lower, now. I lied to my sister.

I squeezed us through the window and carefully closed it behind us. I hoisted her high on my hip and wrapped her blanket over her head.

The streets were empty. I ran to the car and carefully set her down in the backseat. She looked so fragile huddled all wrapped up, with her hair falling into her face and her lips pressed close together.

"Hey." I reached inside the backside and stroked her cheek. "Don't you worry. Your big brother Jesse's here to take care of you."

Her thumb was popped into her mouth and her eyes were

half-closed. "Okay," she mumbled.

I got into the car and drove away.

Thirty-Seven

```
fog (n): 1. a condensed vapor; 2. a state of
         confusion or bewilderment.
```

The fog was so thick that I could barely see the road. I grabbed Bethany's cell phone and punched in Merlin's number.

He answered on the first ring. "Yo. Merle here."

"It's me."

"Hey, pussy. It's so good to hear your voice. You have my payment? You have until tomorrow, you know."

"I'm ready. I have it."

"Really?" He laughed. "No shit? Wow, kid, I didn't think you had it in you."

The tone in his voice made my stomach curl. "Ditch the Scarface routine, already, Merlin."

"Shut up, Jesse."

"I've kicked your ass before and I'll kick it again."

"I wouldn't bet on it," he sniffed.

"So, where should we meet, Beto's?" I was already headed in that direction.

"Beto's? No, man. Meet me out here."

I stiffened. "Bravo Hills? Why? Wouldn't Beto want me to just bring him the money?"

"Nah. I'm handling it for him. I'm like his right-hand guy these days. It's cool."

I didn't want to go out to Bravo Hills. For one, the air clung to the car like a gray blanket. The road out there was a two lane, and people got in accidents all the time in the winter.

Besides that, something was off. But I couldn't put my finger on it.

"No," I said. "Let's meet at the park across from Beto's,"

His voice hardened. "If you don't meet me here at my trailer, the whole deal's off. Do hear me? OFF."

Now I knew something wasn't right. "Fine," I said tightly. "I'll be there."

I clicked off the phone and turned the car around, toward the country. Toward home, or the last place I really called home, anyway.

I drove the car onto the freeway, headed east out toward the trailer park. Cars passed by like ghosts in the mist as we made our way further and further out of town. The cab was dark and quiet.

"Jesse?" Pony called in a small voice from the backseat. "I gotta go potty. Are we almost to the surprise?"

Damn. I really didn't want to take Pony out there, so close to Merlin. I glanced back at her and smiled bravely. "Almost, okay? First we have to play a little hiding game. Can you do that, Pony? If you can, I'll stop at McDonald's and get you a caramel sundae."

"With nuts?"

"Sure, honey. With nuts."

But the truth hit me like a punch in the gut.

I didn't even have enough money to buy her a sundae. She had no extra clothes, not even a toothbrush. How in the hell was I going to make it all the way to Arizona? How were we going to survive?

I'd have to take a hundred from Merlin. He'd just have to deal with it.

We crossed the bridge over the river. I couldn't even see the banks, or the orchards that flanked the sides. I saw nothing but white, endless white, and the occasional passing of another car. Finally, I saw the turnoff. I slowed and drove down the narrow dirt road.

"It's scary out here, Jesse. I want to go home." Pony's voiced trailed over the backseat. We were now a fourth of a mile from Bravo Hills.

11:10pm.

If the Websters weren't home already, they would be at any moment. They'd call the cops, and... We needed to get this done and get out of town, now.

My mind spun. "Guess what?" I said brightly. "That's part of the surprise. We're here; we're going to see our old home." I put my blinker on and turned left.

"No," she said, starting to sniffle. "I don't want to go back there. I want to go home, to my mommy and daddy."

I bit my lip in shock. I knew she wasn't talking about Mom and Darryl, and it made me feel light-headed. "But, Pony, we're only going to be there for a little bit—"

"I want to GO HOME!" she cried, now a full-on wail. Her thin shoulders shook with sobs.

My knuckles were white as I clenched the steering wheel, trying to focus on the road. But as I listened to her cry, I felt my chest constrict.

I couldn't take it, anymore.

"Pony," I yelled, hating myself at that same instant. "You're with me, goddammit! I'm your brother—those people are not your parents, do you hear me?"

She continued to wail.

Jesus, I thought, raking my fingers through my hair. *Christ Almighty, I am completely losing it.*

11:13pm.

I drove through the broken down wooden gate that hung the sorry sign that read: *Bravo Hills*. Handwritten below were the words: *Vacancy, inquire at the office.* Thing was, there were always vacancies. I sucked in my breath when I saw Merlin's trailer. The lights were on and the orange El Camino was parked outside.

I parked the car just in front of the sign and jumped in the backseat. "Come here, Pony," I said, reaching for her. I rewrapped the thick blanket around her and brushed the hair out of her eyes. "I'm sorry. I shouldn't have yelled at you. Don't cry," I murmured, trying to reassure myself as much as her. I rocked her, like I did so many times when she was a baby, and kissed her head. "Everything's going to be okay," I said.

My shoulders shook with dry, silent sobs.

Nothing made sense anymore. God, what was I doing?

What was I doing?

The phone rang.

What an idiot. He was so impatient. I picked up the phone to go and yell at Merlin and almost dropped it when I saw that it was the De Leons.

It kept ringing.

My hands shook.

I knew I shouldn't talk to him, but I found myself putting the phone to my ear.

"Hello?" I choked. "Daniel?"

"Jesse. Thank God, it's not too late." He sounded worried as hell. "Where are you, son? Talk to me. What's going on?"

Pony still cried beside me. "I don't know anymore. Look, I'm in some serious shit, Daniel. I owe some bad people a lot of money." I took a ragged breath. "I'm real sorry I took Nate's guitar. I want you to know that."

"Jesse, I don't care about the guitar. We can work things out. Let me help. Tell me where you are."

"Jesse," said Pony beside me, tugging on my arm. "I still need to go potty."

I began to feel panicky. "You can't call the cops. Please, Daniel, listen to me. Let me just do this and it will keep us all safe."

"Jesse, *where are you?* Is that Pony with you? If it is, son, you could be breaking the law. You don't need to get into any more trouble. Let me help. Let me come and get you."

I let out a thin, strangled laugh. "Breaking the law? You have no idea. My whole life has been breaking the law. It's too late for me."

"It's never too late," he said quickly, keeping his voice calm. "Never. Just remember that. I believe in you, Jesse. I believe in who you are. And you aren't this. It's never too late."

Who are you?

I heard Abuelo's voice, floating from deep within the recesses of my mind.

I held my sister's body close to me, smelling the scent of her clean hair. God, I loved her, and I wanted her safe.

"Okay," I whispered into the phone, the tears running down my face. "Okay. We're coming home."

The door to Merlin's trailer opened, the light from inside pouring out like a lighthouse beam in the night.

"What the fuck are you doing?" he shouted, walking toward the car. "You've been parked there for five minutes. Come on in and let's do this."

With one swift motion, I buckled Pony in tight, all the time keeping my eyes on Merlin. He wasn't holding his gun.

"Hold on," I whispered to Pony. "I'm going to be driving very fast."

"Okay," she whispered back. Her eyes were like saucers.

I crept back into the driver's seat and started the car. Gunned it and said a prayer.

"What the fuck?" I heard Merlin shout behind me. "Get your ass back here!"

"There's been a change of plans," I said, as I peeled down the road.

Thirty-Eight

panic (n): a sudden, overpowering fright.

We raced through the fog. I drove silently, not daring to look in the rearview mirror to see if Merlin was following me yet. The radio still played a scratchy version of White Christmas, the Bing Crosby one. I flicked it off. The cell phone rang.

Pony lifted her head and popped her thumb out. "Phone's ringing," she lisped.

I saw the lights on the face flash. Missed call from Daniel.

"Yeah, Pone." I jerked my head back toward her, struggling to keep my face calm and pleasant. "I'm not going to get it. I'm going to concentrate on driving."

"To the surprise?"

"Yup, that's it. To the surprise."

What surprise we had waiting for us, I didn't know. I was sure by now that Daniel had called the cops, and probably the Calloways, too, if they hadn't figured out already that she was missing. They would be freaking out.

I'd do time, for sure. I was already prepared for it. Theft, kidnapping, drug charges, God knew what else.

I planned on telling the cops the whole thing, from the day I took Beto's package, to losing it, to Merlin blackmailing me. Everything. Because I had to make sure that he would be locked up, and Beto too, and I knew I couldn't survive in juvie without knowing that Pony was safe.

I'd probably never see her again.

Don't screw it up now, Jess. Get her safe, first.

One small comfort was that the streets were empty this time of night. I was careful to drive the speed limit, and I didn't want to get pulled over before we made it safe back to the Webster house.

"Jesse!" Pony burst into a fresh set of tears. "I wet my pants."

"No, no," I said in a reassuring voice. "It's okay. We'll get you fresh clothes when we get to the surprise."

"I'm all wet," she cried, choking out tears.

"I know, baby. I'm sorry." I furrowed my brow and checked the rearview mirror. It still looked clear, thank God. "It's okay."

I turned down the country road that led to the De Leon's. I flooded the gas as I passed Hailey's house. The revving of the car's engine caused the horses in her front pasture to rear their heads as we sped past.

The sound of a car horn blared behind us.

Holy shit, it was Merlin. How did he catch up so fast? I wondered, in a split-second.

I gunned it.

"Jesse, I'm scared," cried Pony.

I peeled into the De Leon's long driveway. All the lights were on in the house and floodlights shined on the front lawn. The Calloway's SUV was parked in front. I slammed the car into park, raced around to Pony's side, and flung open her door. When I unbuckled the belt, I could feel her wet bottom through the blanket.

I grabbed her and made a break for it. I could see the Daniel and Bethany and the Calloways standing at the front door. Mrs. Calloway was wrapped in a bathrobe, sobbing, as Bethany hugged her and patted her back.

"He's coming!" I yelled. The distance to the house seemed like forever and my legs pumped as fast as they could.

"Jesse!" Daniel screamed. "Hand her to me and get inside, hurry!" He held his arms out and ran toward me.

Just as that instant, the orange El Camino skidded onto the lawn and ricocheted against Bethany's Corolla, denting the front. Merlin backed it up and rammed it again, causing sparks to fly out in tiny, comet-like bursts. The car jerked to a stop and Merlin roared out, pointing his gun at my head.

"Stop right there, Jesse." he said in a hoarse voice. "I'll kill her, man, you know I will. I'll fucking kill her."

I stood frozen with my back to Merlin. I could see the horrified expressions of the Calloways, Daniel, and Bethany as they faced me. I swallowed the bile down in my throat and slowly turned around.

Dixon, another stoner friend of Merlin's, climbed out of the passenger side and walked toward Merlin with his hands out. "Merle," he said in a low voice. "We don't need it that bad. She's just a little kid, man."

"Quiet, Dixon!" Merlin barked, spittle flying from his mouth. "This fucker has it coming to him."

Merlin was tweaking hard. His eyes were wild, crazed, and his long hair was so greasy that it was plastered into limp clumps on either side of his head. His face was covered in pus-filled sores, and his hands shook as he held the gun at my face.

I exhaled shakily. "If you want the money, it's yours. I've got it right here, in my back pocket."

His eyes were so dilated that I could barely see his irises. They were cold and dead, almost like he was a different person. "No. Too late. I'm taking the money, but I'm taking Pony with me, too."

Ohmygodnotthatanythingbutthat…

"What? Hell, no."

"Come on, Pony." Merlin gestured to her with the gun. "Get in the car. We're going for a little ride."

"No! Jesse," whimpered Pony, burying her head into my neck. She was growing heavy, but I didn't dare let go. I clutched her firmly to me.

I lifted my eyes to meet his empty gaze. "Since when does Beto kill kids, Merlin? What's he gonna say about you harming a little girl in his name?"

"Beto?" Dixon looked from me to Merlin. "…Did Beto put you up to this? I thought you said he was locked up for years."

I felt my heart constrict as everything became suddenly, perfectly clear.

"He's locked up?" I asked Merlin, in a tight voice.

"Shut up, Jesse."

"So, when did that happen? This has nothing to do with Beto, does it? I bet he doesn't even know I'm back. You've been blackmailing me on my own, this whole time."

The look on Merlin's face told me I was right. His teeth clenched into a snarl, and he took a step forward. "I paid for your mistake,

Jesse," he said, arching his neck so I could see the scar on his cheek. He held the gun shaking in front of him. "In more ways than one."

"Just take the money, son." Daniel had crept closer, with his hands stretched out. "You don't have to hurt these kids, too."

"Don't come any closer!" Merlin screeched, waving the gun at Daniel. "I'll shoot!"

I heard the sound of cars racing down the street. There was no sound of sirens, but I knew that it was the cops. I closed my eyes.

"Fuck!" screamed Merlin. "Fuck! Give me the money!"

I whipped it out of my back pocket and flung it to Merlin. He kept the gun pointed and picked the bundle of cash up. "Now give me the kid." He motioned for Pony. "Now!" I heard the sound of sobbing from the Calloways.

"Pony," I whispered into her ear. "I'm going to set you down, honey, and then you run to Daniel. Okay?" She nodded.

"Look, Merlin," I said slowly. "Watch me. I'm just going to set her down for a minute." I bent down and rested Pony carefully on the ground.

Three cop cars sped down the road and up the driveway. Merlin turned his head, and in that brief instant, I whipped my body in front of her and pushed her behind me.

"Go!"

He turned back around, saw her running, and pointed the gun in her direction.

"No!" I shouted, and ran in front of him, making my body as big as possible to block his shot. "No!" I heard myself scream again, and I ran toward him, and lunged for the gun.

There was a loud crack, and then I felt an intense pressure in my gut. Three more cracks erupted from somewhere in the distance.

My legs buckled beneath me, and I felt myself falling, falling toward the damp ground. *It's so cold*, I thought, as my face touched the frosted, deadened blades of grass. I felt wetness leaking from me, and touched my stomach. My shirt was sticky and warm and I smelled the sweet saltiness of blood. Screams and shouts and the sound of running floated all around me.

I struggled to see if Pony was safe, but my eyes wouldn't focus.

So this is it, I thought, as my vision flooded with black, fuzzy splotches.

After everything, this is it.

Thirty-Nine

choose (v): to select freely.

When I came to, the first thing I smelled was antiseptic. I heard the low buzzing of machinery: orderly, calm, and regular. The sounds of an intercom paging someone in the hallway. Muted footsteps and the purposeful rustle of surgical scrubs. The squeak of the rubber mattress beneath the thin cotton sheets and the itch of tape holding plastic tubing as it snaked through my nose.

But most of all, I felt pain.

Getting shot in the gut does not feel too good. In fact, it feels like real frickin' hell. I opened my eyes and saw the wound, covered completely with bandages and gauze. A bag of fluid dripped into a needle taped to my arm.

The thought came to me in a quick flash. *I'm alive.*

I groaned.

"Jesse?"

I cricked open an eye. Daniel sat hunched in a vinyl chair next to the window. He huddled under a blanket.

I managed to open the other eye. "What are you doing here?" I expected to see Theo and maybe a police officer, but Daniel was the last person I thought I'd see.

"I've been here the whole time. Bethany, too." He smiled, the circles a dark gray beneath his eyes. "She even insisted on us sleeping here. She's in the cafeteria right now."

His dreads were all frizzed-out and his beard sported several days' growth. His eyes looked bloodshot from lack of sleep. "You look like shit."

A low laugh rumbled in his chest. "I should bring you a mirror."

My emotions felt scraped raw looking at him. I met his gaze. "I just figured, after what I did, that you'd never want to see me again."

He got up, walked swiftly to my side and sat on the edge of the bed. "Jesse," he said. "You shouldn't figure. What happened was bad, really bad, but in the end, you came back. You made the right decision. I prayed that you would." His hazel eyes crinkled at me. "What you did was very brave."

"But I kidnapped Pony. Stole Nate's guitar, Bethany's car. God, it got wrecked didn't it? Merle ran into it."

He considered. "Yeah, Bethany's not too happy about her Toyota, I'll admit. And we can talk about the guitar, later."

"I hocked it. I'll get it back." I scrunched up my eyes. "God, I'm such a fuck-up."

"Jesse, look at me." I gave him a glance and his mouth turned up at the corners. "Don't you know what you did? You saved Pony's life."

My head began to clear. My memory was so fuzzy, and I remembered things in bits and pieces: Pony's wet pajama bottoms, the sound of bullets, falling, the ambulance ride, the blood. My eyes widened, and I struggled to sit up — *there were three more gunshots, please no, there were three more gunshots…*

"Pony?" I asked, wincing, because it hurt to take a breath.

"No, no." He patted my arm. "Don't worry. She's fine."

I sucked in another breath as I struggled to speak "Did she… Did he—?"

"No, no. Jesse," he interrupted, smiling gently at me. "She's completely fine."

I sank back into my pillow. *She's completely fine, he said. Nothing else mattered. At least I didn't screw that part up. She was alive.*

"You could have died, you know. If that bullet hit a centimeter or two to the left, it would have burst an artery. As it is, you lost your appendix. Jesse, you were very, very lucky." He hesitated. "I'm afraid you're going to be in here for a while. You'll miss Christmas."

"What about Merlin? Is he arrested?"

He cleared his throat. "Your, ah, friend, Merlin. I'm sorry, Jesse. But, the police…they shot him. He's gone."

The other gunshots.

I felt tears prick my eyes. I don't have any clue as to why, but hearing that Merlin was dead made me feel sad, really sad. I guess it was because we had known each other for so long, and even though he was for the most part a major screw-up, that guy out in front of the De Leon's house holding a gun in my face wasn't the guy I knew for all those years.

The only way it could make sense was that it was the drugs that finally overtook him, and changed who he was.

I nodded, closing my eyes. "Okay."

I wondered what his dad would do, who he would play World of Warcraft with, now that his son was dead. He hated driving, because it always bugged his leg. Who would get his groceries? Buy his pot?

Daniel watched me patiently. "I should let you rest."

"No," I said, the sharp intake of breath causing a fresh cascade of agony weave through my gut. "Please, don't. How long have I been here?"

"Three days."

My eyelids flew open. "No shit?"

Another wry grin. "No shit." He hesitated. "Jesse, we'll need to talk, about everything, because there's a lot I need to explain, and there's a lot you'll need to be telling people."

I had been waiting for this. "I already know. I'm in deep, and there's no getting out of it."

"You know, sometimes you just have to wade through it. Face it."

"I know. No more running. Not anymore."

Forty

truce (n): a suspension of fighting.

A couple days later, some detectives came by. They asked me a bunch of questions about Merlin, Beto, and that package they wanted me to deliver so many months ago. Turns out Karat got arrested not long after he lifted it from me, and they had been trying to tie that package to Beto this whole time.

"If you're able to testify against him," said the taller, thinner detective, "then we could get you out of serving any time in juvie. You could be a free man."

There was no option. I had to tell the truth, and come clean, whatever the consequences. "I'll do it," I said.

I guess once Beto landed in jail, Merlin got himself in a mess of trouble with the bigger drug dealers Beto was hooked up with in Mexico. He never was that good with money and got in over his head. Owed those guys a lot of money. In Merlin's eyes, blackmailing me was his ticket out of hot water.

Daniel and Bethany visited me every day in the hospital. They didn't have to, but I was grateful. One day, Bethany handed me a package before she left.

"What's this?" I asked. Christmas still wasn't for a couple of days.

She tucked her hair over her ear and smiled. "I thought I'd give you one of your presents a little bit early. Something to keep you occupied, I figured."

I broke through the wrapping. Three different sketchpads and a brand-new set of charcoals. "Thanks," I said, as I fingered the blank pages and sharp points of the pencils. "Thanks a lot."

"Maybe you'll get inspired," she said as she squeezed my shoulder.

*   *   *

Christmas Eve.

I kept the TV off and spent the whole day sketching. It started out being just one picture, but as the minutes turned into hours, I kept filling up page after page of pictures that crowded my mind.

It gave me time to think, to process everything that had happened. I drew so much that my hand cramped from use. By the time the orderly came with lunch, the heel of my hand was smudged gray.

"Hey, Eileen," I said, eyeing the steaming tray covered with stainless-steel plate covers. "Whatcha got there today?"

Eileen was a grandma type, with a thick long white braid trailing down her back and a big puffy mole above her lip.

"Jesse, Jesse, Jesse," she said with a grin. "My biggest fan. I never did see someone with an abdominal injury enjoy food so much."

I sniffed, trying to guess what was inside. "Ham today? No, turkey, I think. You got those little tapioca cups in there for me?"

She chuckled. "Maybe I do, maybe I don't. You'll just have to find out, won'tcha?"

She opened the trays, refilled my water, and pulled the table over across my lap. Sure enough, it was turkey with thin, congealed gravy, and smushy green peas. Something resembling stuffing was clumped over to the side. Piled up on the tray were four tapiocas.

Heaven on a plate. I looked up at her and grinned. "Thanks, Eileen. You're the best."

"Yeah, yeah." She winked. I could see dark hairs growing out of the mole. "I bet you tell that to all of the ladies. See ya later," she added, shutting the door behind her.

Tim was right about those hospital puddings. They were pretty damn good, especially the tapioca ones. I liked chewing on the little rice thingies the best.

What he wasn't so right about, however, were the nurses. They were all nice, more or less, but none I'd want to look at all day, if you know what I mean. Maybe things were different in Los Angeles, but I had yet to come across a single hot one in Truckston.

I pulled off the top of one of the tapiocas and licked it.

"Knock-knock."

Theo's face popped inside of the privacy curtain. His cheeks were ruddy and his curly beard was thick, making him look like the Mexican version of Santa Claus.

"Hey, Theo. What the hell? Since when do social workers work on Christmas Eve?"

"Good to see you, too, Jesse." He pulled up a chair over to my side and readjusted his sweater. "Merry Christmas and all that."

"Yeah." I managed a faint smile.

"You hanging in there?"

"Trying to." I took a large bite of tapioca. The cool sweetness felt good as it went down my throat. I caught Theo eyeing my puddings. "Go ahead. Have one."

He laughed and picked one up. "I haven't had one of these since grade school. You look good," he added. "How much longer do you have in here?"

"The doctors say another week or two. Maybe I'll get out before New Year's, if I'm lucky." Besides the initial loss of blood, and removal of my appendix, the docs said that my injury wasn't too serious. I was recovering pretty quickly, maybe a little too quickly. Part of me didn't want to face life outside of the predictability of the hospital routine.

"I hear you have court next month. We're all rooting for you, Jess."

"Thanks. I'll need it."

I noticed him fidgeting and glancing over at the door.

"What is it?"

"Well…"

"Come on, Theo. You're a terrible liar."

A slight smile crept on his face. "You have visitors."

"Who?" I sat up a little, craning my neck toward the door.

"Pony."

My body chilled. "No. I don't want to see her," I said quickly. "Not yet. Not like this. Tell her to go home."

"Why not?" He pressed his lips together. "Look, she's been dying to see you. She's been asking about you all—"

"Jesse!" I heard her voice first, and then saw her as she ran to the foot of my bed. She was dressed in a red velvet jumper and ribbons separated her hair into two neat, French braids. She started climbing up on my bed.

Mrs. Calloway followed behind her. She moved stiffly, carefully, as she pulled her down. "Crystal, honey. You need to be careful of Jesse's injury. You can't climb up on him." Her eyes met mine, and she gave me a quick, polite nod.

"Okay." She slid down, and stood next to my head, her blue eyes big and luminous as she took in the tubes, the hospital bed.

I tried to blink away the stinging in my eyes. "Hey Pone." With my free hand I touched her soft, round cheek. "Merry Christmas."

"You got shot." Pony threaded a hand through the slats and touched my arm. Her fingers were soft and warm. "You had blood on you."

Mrs. Calloway walked over and smoothed Pony's hair. "She's-she's been having nightmares. Of you getting hurt. It's been keeping her up — the nightmares. She thought you were dead, and the therapist said that if she saw you...if she saw you—" Her hand fluttered to her mouth.

There was a long, awkward silence.

"Can she sit next to me?" I asked. "It's okay, I promise she won't hurt me, if I can make room." She nodded, and I scooted over with some difficulty and patted the empty space beside me. Pony scrambled up and nestled next to me. With the TV on, it reminded me of the last night we spent together, watching Baywatch reruns and eating ramen noodles.

"We would have come sooner, but I didn't want Pony seeing you with all those tubes in you. I was afraid it might scare her."

Mrs. Calloway patted an imaginary loose strand of her hair back into her ponytail.

Pony touched my IV. "Mama said you looked real sick."

"I know. I felt real sick. But I'm getting better now."

I squeezed Pony's hand and touched the lace of her cuff. "Listen," I said in a calm, gentle tone, "Merlin's gone now. He can never hurt me, or you, ever again."

"'Cause he died?"

I closed my eyes briefly. "Yeah. Cause he died. The police got him because he was trying to hurt us."

She nodded knowingly. "That's what my Mama Karen said. Merlin became a bad guy."

"That's right, Pone. Merlin became a bad guy."

Mrs. Calloway cleared her throat. "Crystal, why don't you tell Jesse what we're doing for Christmas?"

Pony got all excited. "We're going to church in a little bit. Do you like my new dress? And then we're having dinner with my Nana and Papa, and then tomorrow, Jesse, guess what?"

"No, tell me. What?"

She whispered into my ear. "Santa Claus is going to come."

I opened my mouth in mock disbelief. "No."

"Yes! I'm not kidding you! He's really going to come." She laughed, it was high-pitched and melodious, and then sighed, resting back against my shoulder. "Ooh!" She sat up straight. "We got you presents! Mama, can you get them?"

Theo gave Mrs. Calloway a significant glance. He held out his hand. "You know what? I think they're still in the hallway, with your dad. Why don't you come with me and we'll get them?"

She watched them leave the room and turned back around,

forcing a smile. "I hear you get to go home pretty soon. That will be nice."

"You know — I'm sorry, Mrs. Calloway. For everything."

She adjusted her pink sweater and fingered her pearl earrings. She looked up, her eyelashes fluttering as she struggled to compose herself. "It's just — you broke into our house. I went into her room…she usually kicks off the blankets when the heat comes on so I usually have to recover her — and… and she was gone. Gone."

I didn't know what to say. She cried quietly as my oxygen tank hummed and the television droned in the background.

Mrs. Calloway lifted her eyes to mine. "We're not pressing charges; I wanted you to know that—"

"I don't care," I said swiftly. "I mean, you should, I broke in—"

"We're not pressing charges. It's already done." She sighed. "We understand, Jesse. We're trying to, at least."

And then as I watched her, trying to be civil, trying to face me — I finally got it. Even though we were enemies, in a way, we were still on the same side. We both loved Pony.

Pony and Theo came back in with two wrapped presents. Pony lifted them up on my bed, and we opened the first one together. It was a new outfit: jeans and a plaid shirt.

I glanced at Mrs. Calloway, we were still being extra careful with each other. "You didn't have to do that," I said to her. "But, thanks."

"You like them?" She smiled. "If they don't fit, there's a gift receipt in the bag."

"No, they're perfect."

"This one's from me." Pony pulled the tissue out of a red bag pulled something out. "I picked it out all by myself."

It was a plastic My Little Pony, like the kind I had given Pony when she was little. It was pink, with sparkles and hearts on the butt.

"Her name is Pinkie Pie," Pony said breathlessly. "She's my favorite. Do you like her?"

I kissed the top of her head. "I love her," I said sincerely. "But are you sure you don't want her for yourself?"

"No," she said, shaking her head. "If you keep her, then it will be like always having me with you. You'll always have a Pony."

"That's that best present ever," I said, giving her a squeeze. "I'll keep it close, always." I reached behind me and grabbed Pony's present off the side table. "Here, I got you a present, too. I made it. I didn't wrap it, though." I handed it to her.

"Mama, look, Jesse made me a book!" It was one of the sketch pads. I had drawn on almost every page.

On the first page, I had written: *Pony's Story*. Inside I drew for her everything I knew, about our life. The first picture was the familiar view of the mountains from the trailer, with the river below. I drew sketches of Mom, Darryl, me, Pony, anything and everything I could remember. I tried to draw all the happy memories, like the time I caught Pony a baby bunny, and we kept it for a while, feeding it fresh grass and oatmeal, or the time we went to the Fair, and I took her on the merry-go-round for the first time.

Pony started flipping through the book "Look — it's Merlin, and Mommy, and—"

Mrs. Calloway stood up and gently took it from Pony's hands. She slowly thumbed through the pages. "This is great, Jesse. I had no idea you were so talented. Oh." Her voice caught as she came upon a picture of Pony with the Calloways. Pony craned her neck to look. "Oh, Mama," she said, pointing. "It's you and Daddy Steve."

"I only drew from memory," I said, feeling my cheeks grow hot. "It's not very good."

Theo gave me a hesitant smile. "Maybe we need to have her look through this with her therapist, if you don't mind."

"I just wanted her to remember, her life. Me."

Mrs. Calloway's eyes filled with tears. "She'll do more than remember, Jesse. I want her to be able to see you. It's what's best for her. I'm sorry, but it took me a while to see that."

It took me a while, too.

Forty-One

adoption (n): the act of taking someone as
one's own child.

On the day of Pony's adoption, Daniel asked if I wanted to go fishing. I had never fished before, never even seen him fish, either, but I figured that it would be nice anyway to spend the day on the river. He asked if I knew of a good place, so I mentioned the old swimming hole right up from Bravo Hills.

Daniel looked at me sideways but didn't say anything. He's cool like that, cool enough to know when to say something and when to just be quiet. We drove out there, not talking much, just enjoying the drive and the songs on the radio and the wind that came in through the windows and messed up our hair. It was an early spring day, and all the trees and little plants were starting to burst open with fresh green buds.

When we were nearing the turnoff for Bravo Hills, I shrugged my shoulders real casual like and said, "Want to see where I grew up?"

He nodded but didn't make a big deal, just slowed down and turned off the road.

It was a ghost town like always during this time of day, but I couldn't help just drinking it all in.

We passed Merlin's trailer. Obviously Merlin wasn't inside but still, there sat the orange El Camino, pulled up right alongside of the front door. I knew without checking that his dad was probably inside getting high and playing X-Box. It made me kind of sad.

He scanned the trailers. "Which one was yours?" he asked.

I pointed. Our trailer was still there, perched on the very edge of the park, with a view of the river down below. Now there were yellowed curtains in the front and tricycles and plastic toys piled next to a planter full of dying flowers. A dirty doll in a plastic carriage sat on its side.

At least one little girl lived there.

I stared for a long time. I wondered how messed up that little girl's parents were, if she saw her mom shoot up and if drug addicts partied in her house. I wondered if she had a big brother, or big sister to take care of her, or if she was the one taking care of someone else. I wondered if she ever looked down at the river during sunset, when it was real peaceful-like, with the sun setting and the swallows skimming the insects off the water, and wished that her life could be better.

If she knew what better even was.

"Hey," said Daniel. "You ready to fish?"

"Sure," I said. "Let's go."

I was ready to leave.

* * *

Funny I had been to that fishing hole a million times, but I never actually fished. Some of the trailer park kids and I would swim when it got real hot, but mostly I would go there by myself when I needed time to think and draw.

Daniel showed me how to bait my line. We sat there listening to the river and waiting for the fish to bite. I wondered if Pony had been adopted yet. The Calloways tried to be real nice about it, even invited me to her adoption party, but I didn't want to screw things up for them.

I didn't know how I'd feel, to be honest.

I looked at the river for a long time. The current was strong, and I watched as the rapids broke into white foam over the smooth speckled boulders. Bits of branches floated along the top, moving swiftly, at the mercy of the water, taking them wherever it was going.

Daniel reeled in his line and hoisted up the fishing rod, keeping it taught. He glanced at me. "You all right?"

"I don't know."

"What don't you know?"

The river looked the way I remembered, but at the same time, it was completely different. Everything was different. And it made me feel weird inside, like I shouldn't be there, like it wasn't my river anymore. I shrugged. "Sometimes I feel like I don't know how to do it."

"Do what?"

"This. *Living.* It's all so screwed up." I took a breath, the sage strong and pungent. "Sometimes I feel like I'm too screwed up."

"We're all a little screwed up, Jesse. That's life I guess. But there's a way to make it better."

"How's that?"

"You choose to live — wade through it, every day. Choose it despite all the crap you've been through. You can decide."

I didn't really know what he was talking about but in a way I did. His words brought up images of my life, the ones I wanted to remember: Pony, the way she looked when I made her laugh; the sight of the river first thing in the morning, with the herons flying overhead; Tim, and our friendship. Walter, and the way he stuck his neck out for me out in the orchard. Aurora, the way her lips felt on my mine.

"I guess I can try."

He smiled. "That's all any of us can do." He took a breath. "It's been over six months, and you're doing well, living with us. Catching up in school, making some friends. Jesse, you've come a long way."

"Thanks."

"You're a fine young man."

A man.

A big fat tear slid down my face and I hastily wiped it away. A fine young man.

"You can say that, after all that shit I put you through?"

He laughed, that deep and rumbly laugh that he did when something was really funny. "Yeah, Jesse. I can still say that."

We let the silence fall between us, the way we did when we were done playing guitar, out in the backyard. But it was a nice silence, a good silence.

"So?" He lifted an eyebrow. "How about it?"

I felt the corners of my mouth tug, not completely understanding. "How about what?"

"Bethany and I have been talking. How about staying with us?

Like for good?" His face stayed neutral. "You know, if you want."

That deep ache, the one I felt for the first time when I was eight, sitting on Mandy's lap, tugged within.

I could be your little boy, maybe. Take me away, and I could be your boy.

A part of me would always stay in the trailer park. And I knew, despite wherever I ended up, wherever life would take me, that the part of me that lived there, would never change. It was my past.

It made me who I was.

"I don't know," I said. I shrugged. "That might be cool."

"Yeah?" He shot me a sideways grin. "I think so, too."

Forty-Two

remember (v): to retain in the memory.

It has been a month since Pony's adoption and each day I think my life is getting a little better.

In addition to art class, I signed up to take a technical drawing class at the city college for summer school. Bethany showed my sketches to the art professor there and he thinks that I could have a pretty good shot at getting into Cal Poly's architecture program, if I keep my grades up for my senior year.

I let it slip and called Daniel 'Dad' the other day. He just smiled. Maybe I didn't just let it slip. It was nice calling someone Dad for the first time in my entire life. Trying it on for size.

Daniel and Bethany surprised me one weekend by taking me to the ocean for the first time. It looked exactly like I thought it would, big and blue and alive. Alive, like the way I felt these days. I walked up to the shore and let the water flow over my bare feet as I closed my eyes and listened to the sound of the waves. I decided it was the best sound I ever heard.

The judge commuted my sentence for my part in Beto's drug deal to 100 hours of community service. My lawyer said I got off real easy. I knew I did, because I got off with my life.

Merlin couldn't say as much.

It took a while to make it through those 100 hours, but I did, slowly but surely. The first 50 I worked off cleaning the side of the road with other kids like me. When that gig was over, I signed up for making meals at the local homeless shelter. I knew what it was like to be hungry.

And homeless, for that matter.

*   *   *

The Rescue Mission is located in a big, tall building in the middle of the downtown, and I drive there early on Saturday morning. Old dudes with yellowed, filmy eyes and younger ones who are high as kites loiter around the front door. A tweaker mom no older than Bethany has parked a shopping cart with three snotty-nosed little girls to the side. One, a tow-head with bright-blue eyes, plays with a doll missing a leg and one eye.

"Hi," I say.

She stares at me as I go inside.

Lunchtime is already over. I walk up to the front desk and introduce myself. "I'm here for my community service hours," I say to the lady behind the desk.

She looks at me dismissively through lowered glasses. I see her glance down at my newer jeans, my backpack, my newly cut hair. I can guess what she is thinking: *spoiled suburban kid*. If she only knew the truth.

"Here's your badge, please wear it at all times. It identifies you as a community service worker. We'll log your hours for your probation officer. I'll need that information, too. Go out to the warehouse. You'll be stocking food crates. Ask for a girl named Gabrielle."

I clip the badge on my shirt and walk through the shelter. To the left is a large men's dormitory. It is empty for the day, because they only allow people to come in to sleep at night. On the right is the cafeteria. Several volunteers mop the floor and wipe down the tables. It smells heavily of bleach and the lingering scent of tomato sauce. The scent reminds me of the Hall.

I step outside and around the corner, into the long, metal warehouse. Crates of food are stacked in the corners. On the shelves are rows of cereal, oatmeal, and large 20 pound bags of rice. A small forklift drives through the opened metal door and sets a pallet of crates down on the concrete floor.

To the left of the forklift stands a slim girl with long, dark hair. She carries a clip-board and checks something off with her pen. I walk up to her.

"Hi. I'm Jesse Sampson. I'm here for my volunteer hours."

She keeps her nose buried in her clipboard. Seems like the uptight, prissy type. "Jesse Sampson?" She scans the clipboard until she finds my name and makes a checkmark. "You're late."

I scoff. It's hard to tell, but she can't be much older than me. Maybe my age, even. "I don't think so. They told me to be here by 2:00. It's only 2:10."

She lifts her eyebrows. "Like I said, you're late." She flips her hair behind her and looks up to meet my eyes.

I suck in my breath.

Her hair, that's the first thing I recognize.

Chocolate. Long and brown. So shiny. I thought about that hair more than once during the past year. She has on a light-blue sundress that makes her skin look golden. She looks clean, fresh.

Her eyes widen.

She remembers me.

It's her, the girl from the park, almost a whole year ago.

"Wha—what did you say your name was?" she asks, faltering a little. She holds the clipboard tightly to her chest.

"Jesse. Jesse Sampson." I put out my hand and she takes it. It is soft and cool and I stand there shaking it until I know I need to let go. "Nice to meet you," I say.

She stifles a smile. "Nice to meet you too," she says, slightly dipping her head. "I'm Gabrielle."

"Gabrielle. That's a nice name."

"Thanks." She withdraws her hand, coloring a bit. She composes herself. "Okay, today you'll be helping to organize the incoming food. We've had several new shipments of donations already. You'll be busy most of the afternoon. Think you can handle that?"

I nod slowly. "I can handle that."

I catch a whiff of her hair. It doesn't smell of chocolate but vanilla.

That's nice, too.

"Well." She notices that I am still staring at her, and her eyes twinkle. "I'll get you started. Shall we go inside?"

We shall, I think.

And so it goes.

DID YOU KNOW?

DID YOU KNOW?

- In the U.S. 408,425 children are living without permanent families in the foster care system.
- Through no fault of their own, these children enter foster care as a result of physical abuse, sexual abuse, neglect, or abandonment.
- The average child waits for an adoptive family for more than three years.
- Forty percent of all foster youth are between the ages of 13-20 years of age.
- Only 50% of all foster teens will receive a high school diploma.
- Only 10% of former foster youth will attend college, and of that 10%, only 3% will graduate.
- More than 20,000 children each year never leave the system -- they remain in foster care until they "age out."
- 50% of former foster youth will be homeless during their first two years after exiting foster care.
- Many of these homeless youth will turn to prostitution as a means to support themselves.
- 60% of girls become pregnant within a few years after leaving the foster care system.
- 50% of youth leaving foster care are unemployed.
- 33% will receive public assistance.
- Thirty percent of the homeless in America and some 25 percent of those in prison were once in foster care.

WHAT CAN YOU DO?

- Adopt.

- If you can't adopt, consider becoming a foster parent.

- If you can't become a foster parent, consider helping in other ways:

  o As a CASA volunteer: National CASA
    CASAforChildren.org/Adulthood

  o Consider providing respite for a foster family. Please check your local foster and/or adoption agencies.

  o Provide a foster teen a job.

  o Donate items such as clothing, toys, or school supplies to your local foster/adoption agency.

  o Consider becoming a Big Brother or Big Sister.

ADDITIONAL RESOURCES

National Suicide Prevention Hotline
1 (800) 273-8255
National Suicide Prevention Lifeline
Hours: 24 hours, 7 days a week
Languages: English, Spanish
www.suicidepreventionlifeline.org

Covenant House
Covenant House was founded in 1972 with the simple, profound mission to help homeless kids escape the streets. Today they are the largest privately funded charity in the Americas providing loving care and vital services to homeless, abandoned, abused, trafficked, and exploited youth.
www.covenanthouse.org

Childhelp National Child Abuse Hotline
1-800-4-A-CHILD (1-800-422-4453)
The Childhelp National Child Abuse Hotline is dedicated to the prevention of child abuse.
https://www.childhelp.org/hotline

Child Welfare Information Gateway
This website provides a wealth of resources for foster youth and the adults who support them. It includes information on scholarships and tuition waivers they might be eligible for.
ChildWelfare.gov

Foster Care Alumni of America

FCAA is a national nonprofit founded and led by alumni of the foster care system. Their mission is to connect foster kids with the alumni community and to transform foster care policy and practice.

FosterCareAlumni.org

Adult Survivors of Childhood Sexual Abuse | RAINN

Rape, Abuse & Incest National Network

https://www.rainn.org/get-info/effects-of-sexual-assault/adult-survivors-of-childhood-sexual-abuse

National Resource Center for Youth Development

NRCYD's overall goal is to build the capacity of States and Tribes to provide high quality services to their youth in out of home placements, former foster youth and other youth in at-risk situations.

http://www.nrcyd.ou.edu

Foster Club

FosterClub is a blog outlet that empowers young people to share their stories, which leads to policy changes that improve educational opportunities and stability for foster youth.

https://www.fosterclub.com

Aspiranet

Aspiranet is a state-wide foster family and adoption agency. For more than 35 years, Aspiranet has been dedicated to creating permanent, lifelong connections for children and families located in California. Aspiranet's 35 core family support programs in 44 locations are run by over 1,100 compassionate employees committed to strengthening and empowering communities through the Aspiranet network.

http://www.aspiranet.org

ACKNOWLEDGEMENTS

I'd like to thank everyone along the way who helped make this book possible. What started out as a tiny seed of a story, gestating for many years in my imagination, came to fruition when I joined a writing class we ended up calling The Mondays. Profound thanks to Bonnie Hearn Hill, my literary fairy godmother and dear friend, for always believing in my writing, and being my ultimate cheerleader. To all The Mondays, my old writing buddies, thank you for sharing your stories and hearts with me, I miss you all. And to Meredith and Stacy, I am forever grateful for your critiques, friendship, and steadfast encouragement.

I'd like to thank my entire family, especially my children—Zach, Christian, Kateri, Clare, and Lucie—who tolerate my writing with support and understanding (Pizza…again? Oh, Mom's writing…); my husband, Matt, for his unconditional love and belief in me; my siblings for making my childhood so special; and my parents for giving me a love of books, especially literature. Mom, thanks for teaching me how to write well during my elementary school years. I still get annoyed when people misspell *you're*.

This book has had some fabulous early readers who came to love Jesse and Pony almost as much as I do: Maureen Butler my best buddy forever; Christine Lucas (sister-in-law extraordinaire); my sister Heidi Michael; Lora Rivera, my very first agent, current critique partner and friend; and Lee Misakian. Thank you, you guys are the best.

Special heartfelt thanks goes out to Dan, Joshua, A Book Barn, and everyone else at HBE Publishing. It's been a fun ride so far, and I am so grateful we took a chance on each other. Anne Biggs and Kathy Gorman—I'm glad we're in this together! Thanks Josh for your incredible website expertise. Thanks to Kyle Lowe (kylelowefilms.com) and Michael Barakat (barakatfilms.com) for making the coolest book trailer ever. Thanks to Alice Addington for your fab photography skills and to Grant Addington for being the perfect Jesse.

I have worked with some incredible people in my other job as an adoption social worker who have impressed me with their level of skill and love: social workers, therapists, judges, teachers, lawyers, and some amazing adoptive families. To the adoptive families I have had the privilege of sharing in your journey: thank you. You humble me. To the kids and teens I have worked with: I am in awe of your strength. You guys inspire me.

And last but not least, for all the kids and teens in foster care who are still trying to find their way home: hang in there, you deserve only the best. I will always root for you.

CPSIA information can be obtained at www.ICGtesting.com
Printed in the USA
LVOW07*1657160815

450297LV00001B/1/P

9 781943 050024

Nixon   PZ7.1.L78   Fin   2015